Mademoiselle Giraud,
My Wife

Texts and Translations

Chair
English Showalter, Jr.

Series editors

Jane K. Brown	Rachel May
Edward M. Gunn	Margaret F. Rosenthal
Carol S. Maier	Kathleen Ross

The Texts and Translations series was founded in 1991 to provide students and teachers with important texts not readily available or not available at an affordable price and in high-quality translations. The books in the series are intended for students in upper-level undergraduate and graduate courses in national literatures in languages other than English, comparative literature, ethnic studies, area studies, translation studies, women's studies, and gender studies. The Texts and Translations series is overseen by an editorial board composed of specialists in several national literatures and in translation studies.

For a complete listing of titles, see the last pages of this book.

ADOLPHE BELOT

Mademoiselle Giraud, My Wife

Preface by Emile Zola

Translated and introduced by
Christopher Rivers

The Modern Language Association of America
New York   2002

For information about obtaining permission to reprint material from
MLA book publications, send your request by mail (see address below),
e-mail (permissions@mla.org), or fax (646 458-0030).

Library of Congress Cataloging-in-Publication Data

Belot, Adolphe, 1829–1890.
[Mademoiselle Giraud, ma femme. English]
Mademoiselle Giraud, my wife / Adolphe Belot ;
preface by Emile Zola ; translated and introduced by Christopher Rivers.
p. cm. — (Texts and translations. Translations ; 11)
Includes bibliographical references.
ISBN 0-87352-799-2 (pbk.)
I. Rivers, Christopher. II. Title. III. Series.
PQ2193.B7 M313 2002
843'.8—dc21   2002032586

ISSN 1079-2538

Cover illustration: family photograph provided by Christopher Rivers

Printed on recycled paper

Published by The Modern Language Association of America
26 Broadway, New York, New York 10004-1789
www.mla.org

TABLE OF CONTENTS

ACKNOWLEDGMENTS

Translating this novel, and writing an introduction to it, has long been a dream of mine; doing the work was a genuine pleasure. Much of that pleasure was made possible by the generosity and encouragement of Martha Noel Evans, director of book publications at the MLA, who supported this project from the start. Her engagement, courtesy, and enthusiasm were exemplary, and I am sincerely grateful.

Thanks should also go to the outside readers and to the editorial board of the Texts and Translations series, for their invaluable suggestions and positive responses, as well as to Michael Kandel, for his expert copyediting. Mount Holyoke College granted me the faculty leave during which much of the work was completed.

Many thanks to my generous cousin Georgiana Colvile, who gave me the photograph that serves as the illustration on the cover of this book.

On a more personal note, I would like to thank Ann Cleaveland, whose help allowed me not only to do my work but also to enjoy it. And, as always, incalculable amounts of love and gratitude go to Christopher Miller.

INTRODUCTION

Mademoiselle Giraud, My Wife, a novel about lesbianism by the prolific popular writer Adolphe Belot, began to appear as a serial in *Le Figaro* in late 1869 before being abruptly canceled, allegedly because of public outrage, 22 December. Whether or not this cancellation was a clever marketing ploy orchestrated by Belot, the scandal surrounding it—in conjunction with the provocative theme of the story itself—helped make *Mademoiselle Giraud, My Wife* a huge commercial success when published as a complete novel in 1870. Even the Franco-Prussian War and the Commune did not get in the way of the public's desire to read Belot's shocking book. This desire was not a passing fancy: in the decade after its initial publication, *Mademoiselle Giraud* was reprinted thirty times. Clearly Belot had struck a chord.[1]

Disdained by literary critics but voraciously consumed by large numbers of readers, richly suggestive of contemporary fixations and phobias, and exemplary of many of the literary formulas of the nineteenth-century French popular novel, the novel is truly a popular classic.

Adolphe Belot was born 6 November 1829 in Pointe-à-Pitre (Guadeloupe) and moved to France as a young man to study law. He went on to practice law for a time in

Nancy, relocated in Paris, and became a playwright and novelist.[2] Despite an inauspicious start in the world of letters (his first novel, *Punishment* [1855], and first play went largely unnoticed), Belot experienced success in the theater fairly quickly, with *The Last Will and Testament of César Girodot* (1857). For years to come, he would write plays that were produced in some of the better Parisian theaters.

After the *succès de scandale* of *Mademoiselle Giraud* in 1870, however, Belot was primarily known as a novelist; of the roughly eighty titles of his that are cataloged in the Bibliothèque Nationale de France, more than half are novels. He produced a seemingly endless string of best-selling potboilers, enjoyed by readers who wanted a bit of literary naughtiness without compromising themselves by reading actual pornography. Having highly suggestive titles (*Woman of Fire* [1872], *Woman of Ice* [1878], *Madame X's Mouth* [1882], *Crazed with Love* [1885]) but relatively benign and euphemistic content, Belot's best-sellers were a curious mix of salaciousness and propriety, hitting just the right note that allowed them at once to titillate and remain safe. It was a formula that worked extremely well for Belot and is exemplified by his greatest success, *Mademoiselle Giraud*. Belot's works provoked outrage in more serious but less popular authors such as Flaubert. *Mademoiselle Giraud* was considered a phenomenon offensive enough to merit the explicit opprobrium of the venerable Larousse dictionary itself.[3]

One of the fascinating things about Belot is that he was leading a double life, publishing pseudo-risqué works under his full name while at the same time publishing under the initials A. B. genuinely risqué fiction such as

The Education of a Half-Virgin (1883), *House of Pleasures; or, Gilberte's Passion* (1889), and *The Canonization of Joan of Arc* (1890). One of the very few works by Belot that has been reprinted in recent years and has continued to enjoy some recognition appeared posthumously, under the signature A. B., presumably having been found in his papers after his death: this is the minor erotic classic *Stations of Love* (1896). Perhaps the greatest tribute to his notoriety as a creator of erotica is the fact that well after his death, as late as 1912, books not written by Belot were being published under the pseudonym A. B.

Little information is available about Belot's personal life. He was divorced (a scandal at the time), and it was widely rumored that he and his wife conspired for him to be caught in flagrante delicto with a prostitute so that his wife would be granted custody of their two daughters. It has been suggested that it was at the time of this divorce that Belot began writing erotic fiction. It has also been suggested that the considerable proceeds from both his bodies of work (the pseudo-pornographic and the truly pornographic) were necessary to the maintenance of a rather extravagant lifestyle that included exotic travel and, especially, gambling. His remarkably prolific output of commercially successful works paid off huge gambling debts incurred at the gaming tables of Monte Carlo. He died of a stroke in December 1890, at the age of sixty-one.

Other than these few facts, what little we know about Belot comes to us through his alliance with Emile Zola, whose life and work have of course been exhaustively documented. One can glean, as with a sieve, information about Belot by searching through materials about Zola.

Zola and Belot were acquainted as of 1864–65; between that time and 1870, they exchanged numerous letters. Belot's first professional contact with Zola was when Zola reviewed, favorably, a novel by Belot in the Lyon newspaper *Le salut public*. By 1865, Belot had become influential enough in Parisian theater circles that Zola saw fit to ask him to return the favor, sending him a copy of the manuscript for Zola's first play, *The Ugly Woman*, and asking that Belot persuade the director of the prestigious Théâtre de l'Odéon to produce it (Belot tried, but to no avail).

That same year, Zola's first novel, *Claude's Confession*, was published, as was a play by Belot and Henri Crisafulli, *Monsieur Jouanne's Past*. Both the novel and the play treated the subject of bohemian life, the unconventional lifestyle led by artists and students of the time, to the horror and fascination of the bourgeois. Zola himself, bringing his novel to the attention of a critic, pointed out the coincidence between the two works.

An even closer link between Belot and Zola came about in 1866. Belot and his collaborator Ernest Daudet wrote a novel (first published in serial form in a newspaper), *The Venus of Gordes*, based on an infamous crime reported in the newspapers, the murder of a husband by his wife and her lover. Directly inspired by Belot and Daudet's novel, Zola published his own version of the murder soon after, a short story entitled "A Love Match," in *Le Figaro* on Christmas Eve. The next year, a longer, more polished version of the story appeared as Zola's first truly successful novel, *Thérèse Raquin*. There is an unpublished letter from Belot to Zola written in July 1868, in which Belot discusses the possibility of Zola's adapting *Thérèse*

Raquin for the stage and suggests a close collaboration between the two writers. (Zola's play *Thérèse Raquin* was performed and published for the first time in 1873.)

In 1869, Zola called on his friend Belot once again, this time enlisting Belot in his struggle to have his novel *The Fortune of the Rougons*, the first of the multivolume Rougon-Macquart cycle, serialized in the newspaper *Le siècle*.

Thus, by the time Belot wrote *Mademoiselle Giraud, My Wife*, for which Zola was to provide a preface, there was a web of professional connections between the two men and a pattern of mutual aid in matters of literary business. Zola's essay, written in February 1870 under the curiously transparent pseudonym of "Th. Raquin" and defending Belot from accusations of immorality, was first intended as a newspaper article. But Zola was unable to find a newspaper willing to publish it. Zola thus left the article in Belot's hands, and Belot later had the clever (and no doubt commercially advantageous) idea to use it as a preface to his novel, beginning with an edition in 1879.

Mademoiselle Giraud, My Wife tells the story of Adrien de C., a lonely young engineer who, after a brilliant start to his career in Egypt, decides that the time has come for him to return to France and marry. By chance, he meets Paule Giraud, a beautiful and strong-minded young woman from the best of bourgeois families. From his very first sight of her, Adrien is fascinated.

He discovers that Paule's most intimate friend, without whose company Paule is inevitably bored, is Mme de Blangy, a charming young married—but, oddly, separated—woman he has admired for some time. The two women, he discovers, were best friends in their convent school and have been extremely close ever since. Indeed, Adrien begins his conquest of Paule by discussing the matter with Mme de Blangy. After some hesitation, she concedes that her friend will indeed have to marry at some point and that Adrien is the most suitable man for that purpose. Paule herself remains indifferent throughout the courtship but is willing to comply with her father's wish that she marry Adrien. A marriage is thus arranged.

Following the wedding, Paule refuses to consummate the marriage, offering her husband instead a sisterly friendship. Adrien is understandably baffled by his wife's behavior. Dejected, he leaves her and sets out on an aimless journey. On his travels he meets a man who turns out to be the estranged husband of Paule's friend Berthe de Blangy. It is M. de Blangy who solves the riddle: Berthe and Paule are lesbian lovers and have been since their days together in the convent school.

In the best patriarchal tradition, the two men decide to take their respective wives in hand once and for all. They return to Paris together, abduct the women, and set out on trains headed in different directions, hoping that physical separation will cure their wives. Despite this elaborate scheme, Berthe eventually finds Paule and compels her lover to run away with her. Months later, Paule's mother contacts Adrien, to tell him that Paule is dying in a small village in Normandy and wishes his forgiveness. Adrien rushes to Paule's bedside. Paule acknowledges her guilt and her regret for not having been a real wife to him. Soon after, she dies.

In a bitter and brutal coda, the story ends with a newspaper article describing the drowning death of Mme de

Blangy. It is clear to the reader of the novel that she has in fact been drowned by Adrien. The final words of the novel are a note from M. de Blangy thanking Adrien for having rid the world of the "reptile" that was his wife.

It is noteworthy how unshocking Belot's "shocking" novel about lesbianism is. The controversial and daring subject is treated with great prudishness. Not so much as a kiss is depicted between the women, nor does the term *lesbian* appear (interestingly, it was coined—in its sexual sense—just three years before the publication of the novel). This is in fact a novel not about lesbianism but about a husband's discovery that his wife is lesbian. The title itself suggests this thematic focus: while the first half of it indicates that the book is the story of a woman (*Mademoiselle Giraud*), the second half, with its possessive adjective (*My Wife*), reveals the real preoccupation of the story.

Hence the narrative is filled with its protagonist's bewilderment and fear; neither he nor the reader discovers, until three-quarters of the way through the book, the secret that explains Paule's refusal to allow her marriage to be consummated. Until that point, all that is certain is that there are no sexual relations taking place between husband and wife, leaving both the husband and the reader to speculate on the various possible psychological, physiological, or social explanations. After the moment of truth, bewilderment and fear give way to rage and revulsion on Adrien de C.'s part (and presumably on the part of the typical late-nineteenth-century reader). The story thus follows a torturous path that leads a man to another man, who unveils a despicable truth. It is also the story of a phobia around which one man bonds with another. To dismiss *Mademoiselle Giraud, My Wife* as homophobic is at once an anachronism and an understatement. A closer look at this novel reveals much about the relation between male bonding and the fear of homosexuality.

What makes the homophobia of the work intriguing is its unconsciously homosocial male bonding, the ironically intense and intimate complicity between men around the subject of female homosexuality. Even on the level of its narrative frame, Belot's novel is rife with male-male complicity. Adrien's tale of woe is told to an "intimate friend" from their days together at school, Camille V. When they meet after not having seen each other for many years (in the exclusively male space of a smoking room at a party), Camille cajoles Adrien into telling him the story of his marriage by reminding him of their former intimacy. Above and beyond the flowery and effusive discourse of friendship not uncommon among men in the nineteenth century, Adrien and Camille indeed seem to share an exceptional intimacy, which allows Adrien to tell, for the first time, the story of his failed marriage (with frequent asides to his "dear friend"). The narrative is thus predicated on an intimate same-sex relationship formed in a single-sex school.

The friendship between Adrien and the count de Blangy echoes the friendship between Adrien and Camille. Of Blangy, Adrien says, "We never left each other's side" and describes the count as a "companion" with whom he has "the most charming" relations. Explaining how he could have become so intimate with a total stranger, he says, "I knew only one thing, that my lucky star had given me a most well-bred man, a witty and intelligent man, as my companion. That was enough for me, and I didn't think to find out his name." Adrien tells his story to the count with all the trust and honesty with which he told it to Camille: "I spoke to him frankly, just as I am speaking to you, dear friend." When the time comes for the count to reveal his secret, the secret of their wives' lesbianism, Adrien must beg him for the truth, using their intimacy as his means of persuasion, much as Camille did with Adrien at the beginning of the novel. The last page of the novel ends on a similarly homosocial note, when the count de Blangy thanks Adrien, in the name of all "decent people" (i.e., men of the "better" classes), for having killed his wife, thus making the world safe from the scourge of lesbianism.

The preface that Zola provided for the novel also takes, in a conscious or unconscious echo of Belot, an explicitly homosocial bent. Zola's validation of his friend's novel and its stance on lesbianism can of course itself be interpreted as a homosocial gesture. The preface clearly argues that bourgeois men like Zola, Belot, and, eventually, Belot's readers must band together in order to stamp out lesbianism. Just as the story revolves around complicity and sympathy between Adrien and M. de Blangy and between Adrien and Camille V., so the preface revolves around complicity and sympathy between Belot and Zola and, by extension, between the two authors and their male readers.

Despite the long-established and universally accepted fact that women were among the most voracious consumers of novels, Zola addresses the eventual readers of

Mademoiselle Giraud as if they were all men. The ideal reader of the novel is a stern patriarch who will use it as an admonition to potentially wayward daughters and wives: "Stop hiding his [Belot's] book; put it on your tables, just as our fathers did with the canes with which they whipped their children. And if you have daughters, may your wife read this book before she chooses to have those dear creatures leave her and be sent off to a convent." In a tone of hysteria, Zola then declares to his imaginary male readers, "The debauchery of the ancient world has swooped down on [us]; [our] wives have succumbed to the leprosy of Lesbos."

Lesbianism is thus, in both Belot's novel and Zola's preface, a subject to be discussed, and a social problem to be solved, by men. The homosocial complicity that permits such discussion is, however, never even remotely depicted as a situation that could lead to anything like romantic love or sexual desire. The consummate irony of Belot's novel is that the horrifying story of the intense and dangerous intimacy between two single-sex schoolmates (female) can be told only in the bounds of the intense and safe intimacy between two single-sex schoolmates (male). That irony is underscored by the implied homosociality of Zola's relation to his reader in the preface. But why must intimacy and complicity be feared and mistrusted among women, leading as it can—according to Belot and Zola—to homosexuality, while it is revered among men as a source of healthy comfort, therapeutic bonding, and indeed as the very antidote to homosexuality?

The answer to this question lies in the way in which lesbianism is defined by the novel. Lesbianism, Belot suggests, is the fruit of the unnatural intimacies created by convent schools, in which young girls of various ages live together in promiscuous and insufficiently supervised conditions. Speaking through the character of the repentant Paule (in what can only be described as an improbably parenthetical disquisition on the topic), Belot describes the convent school as a breeding ground for homosexual vice. Reflecting on its origins in the convent, Paule admits that many young girls leave the convent as pure as when they entered it and that convent-schooled girls often go on to become virtuous wives and mothers. Lesbianism among convent-school girls, she specifies, is a matter of chance rather than a general rule. But she also argues that a lonely fourteen-year-old girl away from her mother for the first time is easily seduced by a solicitous, kindly, older girl. This relationship may quickly deteriorate into one of psychological domination, creating a bond that becomes impossible to break. Paule concludes, "More often than not, I'm convinced, men don't ruin women, women ruin each other." Good news (or perhaps not) for male readers.

Convent education was a timely theme in 1870: with the fall of the Second Empire (1852–70) and the rocky transition to a new regime, the Third Republic (1870–1940), things were in flux. A great sociopolitical debate of the period was that of religious versus secular education for young girls. In 1882, after years of strife between church and state regarding education, a law was passed that established once and for all in France a universal system of free, public, obligatory, secular education for both sexes.

Belot is not so prescient as to propose the state-supported, secular education for young girls that would become law. Rather, he suggests instead that the education of girls and young women should be undertaken by mothers, at home. This point is made clear by Paule as she looks back on how she was ruined by the convent:

> "You think that the convent is dangerous for a young girl?"
> "It can be," she answered.
> "What kind of education do you think is better?"
> "The kind one receives from one's mother, at home."
> "It isn't always easy for a mother to raise her daughter well."
> "Well then, she should raise her badly, but she should raise her herself: even if the intellectual training falls short, at least she will have given her daughter a sense of decency."

Maternal home schooling would accomplish two goals, each of which was useful to a patriarchal society. First, that mothers' time and energy would be spent in child-rearing efforts would eliminate many of the opportunities for their straying from the straight and narrow. Second, daughters would be sure to be imbued with family values and would remain under watchful parental eyes; thus would be eliminated any possibility of youthful experimentation or corruption. Home schooling, it seems, would make for a system in which lesbianism was impossible.

Zola was an engaged observer of and participant in the debate on the education of young women, both as an opponent of the convent and as a proponent of secular education. Numerous writings of his, other than the preface to *Mademoiselle Giraud*, demonstrate his belief that convent schools were synonymous with lesbianism, veritable "breeding grounds for homosexuality."[4] Convent education, and specifically its purported link to lesbianism, is explicitly at issue in the lesbian subplots of both *La Curée* (1872), in which there is a lesbian couple of former convent-school friends, one blonde and the other brunette, characters that Zola quite openly borrowed from *Mademoiselle Giraud*, and *Pot Luck* (1882). At almost exactly the same moment as the publication of Belot's novel, Zola wrote a sort of parable for the newspaper *La cloche*, outlining the dangers of convent education (specifically the danger of excessive physical and emotional intimacy among girls), called "In the Convent."[5]

The preface defends Belot against accusations of immorality and sensationalism. In a rather blatant contradiction, Zola at once extols the morality of Belot's project and declares that "the dirty word *immorality* [is] devoid of meaning with respect to literature." He takes readers to task for having bought Belot's book on the assumption that it would provide some titillating glimpse of forbidden love among women. Belot's goal, he tells us, is not to glorify or glamorize lesbianism but rather to expose and stigmatize it. It is in making this point that Zola argues that homosexuality among women (at least those of a certain social class) is inextricably linked to convent education:

> After having read *Mademoiselle Giraud*, I have set as my goal to obtain absolution for Belot for his success. [. . .] Since we still guillotine people in broad daylight, we can surely brand publicly certain vices with a red-hot iron. Don't you realize that you are foolishly and cruelly making a shameless speculator

out of a moralist who has had the great courage to point out one of the scourges of the education of young girls in convents?

He says that the most important lesson a reader can learn from Belot's "useful" novel is that of the dangers of convent education. He hammers home his point one last time at the conclusion of the preface, to make sure that there remains no doubt about his reading of the novel: "And the moral of the story is blinding. When Adrien attempts to save, to redeem, Paule, she tells him with tears in her voice, 'The convent is what ruined me, that communal life with companions of my own age. Tell mothers to keep their children by their sides and not to send them off to be indoctrinated into vice.'"

For Zola as well as for Belot the novel serves not so much to reveal the existence of lesbianism (as he says in the preface, "let's not be hypocritical. We are all very savvy these days") as to explicate its origin, to show how such a thing comes to pass. In keeping with Zola's ongoing fascination with the natural and social origins of human behavior and the interplay between the two, Belot's novel provides an unambiguously environmental response to the question of the origin of homosexuality among women.

To the author of *The Experimental Novel*, Belot's "experiment" had produced conclusive results concerning lesbianism, and those results needed to be communicated to the public. Nowhere in either Belot's novel or Zola's preface does one find the slightest hint that lesbianism, at least among women of the "better" social classes, could spontaneously generate in any context other than that of the convent school or that it could fail to be eradicated through social means (the elimination of such institutions). Lesbianism and convent education are intertwined for Belot and Zola, as are the responses they elicit: homophobia and anticlericalism.

For both writers and their many readers, the interest in discovering the origin of lesbianism is fueled at least in part by the desire to know where blame should be placed. Blame and punishment are the central preoccupations of both the novel and the preface. Lesbianism is represented as a crime against society, and as a crime it must be punished.

Belot's novel contains an explicit plea for the criminalization of lesbianism, a wake-up call to society as a whole but especially to lawmakers who alone have the power to stop the growing scourge of lesbian wives. In the absence of laws against homosexuality among women, husbands must become veritable vigilantes.

France had no laws repressing lesbianism in 1870. Since 1791, there had been no laws forbidding homosexual acts in private between consenting adults of either sex. That women could not be prosecuted for lesbianism, since it was not a crime, clearly left some married men in an uncomfortable position. M. de Blangy, for example, has no legal recourse whatsoever when he discovers his wife's homosexuality. He tells Adrien, "The law [. . .] would obviously have refused me any help; lawmakers have failed to foresee certain misdeeds, which are thus granted impunity. I could barely obtain a separation from the courts: Mme de Blangy's wrongdoings toward me were of such a nature that judges often refuse to admit them as evidence, so that they won't have to punish them." In Belot's story, hapless husbands such as M. de Blangy and Adrien are forced to take the law into their own hands.

Belot's advocacy of hard-line legal repression of lesbianism is completely at odds with the thematic traditions of French fictional narrative, which tends to treat lesbianism with either a winking indulgence or an erotic fascination. Lesbianism appears to have been considered safe to represent in novels, unlike male homosexuality, which, as a genuine taboo, is nearly completely absent from mainstream French literature written before 1900.

There are many novels with lesbian plots or subplots in the French canon that predate *Mademoiselle Giraud*: Diderot's *The Nun* (1796), Balzac's *The Girl with the Golden Eyes* (1834; invoked by Zola in his preface), and Gautier's *Mademoiselle de Maupin* (1835) come to mind. Belot lets us know that he is aware that his work is but a link in a chain of novelistic representations. In Paule and Berthe's love nest on Rue Laffitte, the books on the shelf include these; yet another proof of the extreme naïveté of Adrien is his failure to see the significance of this particular set of titles.[6] What sets *Mademoiselle Giraud* apart from these earlier works is its relative realism. *The Nun* takes place behind the walls of the cloister, in the decidedly non-mainstream and somewhat surreal world of the convent; *The Girl with the Golden Eyes* is full of romantically improbable elements, from Paquita's uncannily beautiful golden eyes to the outlandish coincidence that Paquita's male and female lovers turn out to be brother and sister; *Mademoiselle de Maupin* takes place in a sort of pastoral fairy-tale setting, in a vaguely defined earlier period that clearly has nothing to do with Gautier's own nineteenth-century France.

Its melodramatic style aside, Belot's story takes place in contemporary Paris (the first sentence of the novel sets the stage as follows: "On a certain Tuesday night last February, the part of Avenue Friedland that runs between Rue de Courcelles and the Arc de Triomphe was extraordinarily animated") and in realistic circumstances. All the characters are sociologically plausible, and it is easy to imagine that, absent a few of the more colorful plot twists, such a story could have taken place. Indeed, the realism of *Mademoiselle Giraud* marks a turning point in the history of literary representations of lesbianism in French. While the earlier works are fantastic (on some level or other), those that follow Belot's novel are much more realistic.

It is also interesting to note the emphasis on the topos of male jealousy of lesbianism in several more canonical works. Maupassant's short story "Paul's Wife" (1881), for example, tells of a well-bred young man who discovers the young woman with whom he is infatuated making love to another woman. His disgust and despair lead him to suicide, and his erstwhile lover goes away consoled by her new lover. Given the chronological proximity of Maupassant's work and the rampant commercial success of *Mademoiselle Giraud*, it is possible that the conclusion of Maupassant's story constitutes an ironic wink vis-à-vis Belot: Maupassant's Paul drowns himself rather than his wife's lover, and it is the lesbian couple who walk away at the end of the tale rather than the avenging husband.

More famous is the obsessive jealousy of Proust's narrator Marcel, whose slowly unfolding discovery of his lover Albertine's lesbianism is recounted over the course of three of the volumes of *Remembrance of Things Past* (alluded to in *Within a Budding Grove* [1918], it becomes the thematic centerpiece of *The Captive* [1923] and *The Fugitive* [1925]). As with Belot's Adrien, the lesbianism of a woman with whom the male narrator is in love is a nearly unbelievable, incomprehensible notion that becomes an obsession, as love, desire, and jealousy become indistinguishable in Marcel. Like Adrien, he tries to exercise what physical control he can over the woman he loves. He literally imprisons Albertine, denying her access to any of her female friends other than the one, Andrée, who turns out to have been her lover (thus making the same error in judgment made by Adrien with respect to Berthe de Blangy). Finally, albeit in very different circumstances, the sad tale ends—as does Belot's—when the woman escapes and, having escaped, dies.

The works of Colette that represent lesbianism provide both counterpoints to and echoes of her predecessors. *Claudine at School* (1900) has a complex lesbian plot, set in a girls' school, thus echoing Belot. *Claudine Married* (1902) tells the story of a married woman whose husband not only tolerates but encourages, for voyeuristic purposes, his wife's affair with another woman (who is also married). The husband ends up seducing the wife's lover. Colette's putatively autobiographical Claudine novels are the first mainstream literary representations of same-sex desire between women created by a female author; equally important, they are told from the point of view of a female first-person narrator. It can be argued that Colette's female characters, and their desire for each other, are depicted with greater authenticity than those of Belot or Proust. Colette nonetheless shares the curious back-

and-forth approach to homosexual matters that characterizes most of her predecessors (especially Belot) in the subcategory of novels about lesbianism; she vacillates between world-weary frankness and coy understatement.

That *Mademoiselle Giraud* was perceived by contemporary readers as a realistic work, perhaps even as a sort of novelized version of a sensational story taken straight from the newspaper (à la Belot and Daudet's *The Venus of Gordes* and later Zola's *Thérèse Raquin*), helps explain the success of the novel. Belot surely attempted to titillate his readers with scandalous stories made all the more scandalous by their realism. But that very realism required him to take a clear and harsh stand on the moral question of lesbianism. While it was acceptable for Gautier's bisexual superheroine to go riding off at the end of the novel into an ethereal sunrise, the very believable female characters of *Mademoiselle Giraud* needed to be put to death in order to ease the minds of the readers. Zola's defense of Belot notwithstanding, Belot was something of a literary speculator, risking the fortune of his book on his ability to give the public exactly what it wanted.

Perhaps the most compelling thing about Belot's work is that it is in fact genuinely commercial literature, the content of which is shaped by the author's astute reading of the preoccupations, tastes, and sensibilities of his audience. Belot seems to have calculated what bourgeois readers would find provocative, how far he could go in titillating them, and just what proportion of stern conventional morality had to be added to the mix in order to render the work safe. Such a calculation is the hallmark of the popular novel in nineteenth-century France: sensationalism is a must, but it is required that good triumph over evil in the end. Popular classics such as *Mademoiselle Giraud* can teach us a great deal about the mentality of a particular culture at a particular historical moment. They are formulaic, yes, but those very formulas may paint a clearer picture—albeit in broad strokes—of a period than works whose content was determined by the more idiosyncratic, less commercial, aesthetic vision of a particular novelist. Comparing *Mademoiselle Giraud* with a canonical work of high culture is like comparing a popular television sitcom with a feature film by an auteur filmmaker.

It is important to see Belot's novel in the larger literary context of the popular novel in nineteenth-century France. *Mademoiselle Giraud* is in many ways exemplary of the genre. As it has been defined by the literary historian Yves Olivier-Martin, the popular novel tended to "describe the struggle between Good and Evil in the present, in the society that is contemporary to both authors and readers" (11; trans. mine). This contemporaneity was crucial: readers were invited to imagine a story that might well take place in their midst, a story whose characters were people they might pass on the sidewalk every day, ordinary people in extraordinary circumstances. Belot's novel also exemplifies the popular novel's formula, articulated by Olivier-Martin, of pairing "simplified characters" with "complicated events" (coincidences, chance encounters, improbable plot twists) to create stories "that speak to the imagination, sensibilities and especially the nerves" of their readers (13). Typically, the popular novel was set in Paris, exposing and examining what lay beneath the roiling surface of the developing urban industrial landscape.

Popular novels also tended to revolve around a set of stock characters, of which *Mademoiselle Giraud* presents several: the predatory femme fatale, inevitably punished, usually by death, in the end (Berthe de Blangy); the victimized woman whose virtue has been snatched away (Paule); the hero, who ultimately triumphs (Adrien). The grisly conclusion of Belot's novel is the point at which the novel conforms most closely to the conventions of the popular novel, as defined by Olivier-Martin: "The final appearance of the hero allows for the reestablishment of the order that had been disturbed by the invasion of Evil. Justice is reestablished, a justice that is manifested essentially by gratitude (father and daughter) and revenge. The ending is not necessarily happy" (14).

Belot's heavy use of dialogue, of brief paragraphs (sometimes composed of a simple sentence or two: "She was wrong. I did become a tyrant"), and of expressive punctuation (exclamation points, ellipses) is typical of the nineteenth-century French popular novel. There are two equally valid explanations for this distinctive narrative style: first, the authors of serialized novels were often paid by the line, so it was to their economic advantage to write as many lines as possible; second, this style is the manifestation of the overdetermined link between the popular novel and the theatrical melodrama. As the critic Jean-Claude Varielle has suggested, each of these short dramatic sentences represents a minor theatrical moment that echoes the larger moments of high drama that occur throughout the text, most often at the end of chapters.[7]

Chapters in a novel like Belot's can be read as scenes of a melodrama, the ellipses or exclamation points with which they frequently end signifying the fall of the curtain.

Its conformity to genre convention notwithstanding, *Mademoiselle Giraud* does deviate from the formulas of the French popular novel of the mid to late nineteenth century. The popular novel, targeted at a largely working-class audience, often chose as its heroes and heroines representatives of the working class or the petite bourgeoisie, often pitted in moral and economic struggles against *grand bourgeois* or aristocratic oppressors. One of the functions of the genre, Olivier-Martin has speculated, was to present its readers with a sublimated universe, in which the socioeconomically weak triumph over the strong. Belot's novel, in contrast, takes place among the privileged, aristocrats, and *grands bourgeois* and is devoid of any treatment of class struggle or monetary difficulty. Class is nonetheless at issue in the novel: Adrien specifically says that he is shocked to learn of the existence of lesbianism among women of his own class, and it may be argued that the revelation of the story, for both him and the reader, is less the existence of lesbianism as a human phenomenon than as a possibility among bourgeois and aristocratic women (as opposed to, for example, prostitutes). Indeed, as we have discussed, the subtype of lesbianism treated by Belot, with its origins in convent schools, is by definition exclusive to the "better" classes of society.

The commercial success of *Mademoiselle Giraud* suggests that it was appreciated by readers across a wide spectrum of society, that the specific type of voyeurism it offered varied according to the socioeconomic class of the reader.[8] Readers who could identify, sociologically, with its well-heeled and well-connected characters may have read it almost as a roman à clef, imagining their acquaintances in similar situations. Working-class readers may have read the novel as a means of peering through a gilded keyhole into the lives of the privileged, taking pleasure in the confirmation of the fact that no social circle is immune to vice.

Belot's giving a sociological twist to the popular novel by setting his stories among the privileged was so characteristic of his work that it became something of a trademark. That it proved to be an irresistible combination warrants further scrutiny. The numerous readers of *Mademoiselle Giraud* were, finally, able to have it all. The shocking subject of lesbianism, titillating to both men and women, was rendered completely unthreatening by the stern moralism of the work and presented only under the safe cover of prudish and indirect language, according to the unwritten rules of the genre. This conventional work was, however, enlivened by the extra spice of the enviable social position of his characters. Ultimately, the fundamental irony of the work is also the key to its immense success. By terrifying readers with the story of perverted married women and simultaneously comforting them with the notion that the perversion had a readily identifiable origin, one easily eliminated by social means, Belot wrote in essence the perfect horror story. Berthe de Blangy is a predatory reptile, and contemporary readers no doubt shuddered at the thought of such a creature, but they cheered at her execution by drowning. In short, they could put down Belot's shocking book and still get a good night's sleep.

Notes

[1]The infamy of Belot's novel was international. Translated into English in 1891, *Mademoiselle Giraud* was cited on numerous occasions by reporters and editorialists in conjunction with the sensational Mitchell-Ward lesbian murder case of 1892. The novel was regarded, at least by some, as a scientific study of the phenomenon of lesbianism, one editorialist going so far as to say that Belot had "done more to bring the subject of sexual perversion, as illustrated in the Mitchell-Ward case, before the public than has any scientific physician." Another claimed that in the criminal court of Memphis, where the trial was to take place, Belot's novel would be "the only textbook at hand" (Duggan 24, 181).

[2]The information presented here concerning Belot's life and works, and his association with Emile Zola, has been compiled from several sources: Alexandrian, *Histoire* 238–39 and "Vie" 603–08; Cantégrit; Mitterand 533–35; and Zola (vols. 1 and 3). Other acknowledgments of *Mademoiselle Giraud* as an important moment in the history of literary representations of lesbianism are Faderman 278–81, (on Zola's preface) 283; Foster 81.

[3]Interestingly, Flaubert's outrage was provoked by the huge popularity of Belot's work in comparison to the relative obscurity of Zola's; in a letter to George Sand (1874), Flaubert said, "Into what abyss of idiocy are we to sink? Belot's last book has sold 8,000 copies in a fortnight [as compared to] Zola's 1,700 in six weeks for *The Conquest of Plassans*, and he hasn't had a single article" (Hemmings 83). On the entry in the Larousse dictionary, see Nathan 183.

[4]Schor notes that in Zola's novels the word *pensionnaire* ("convent-school girl") "is another way of saying lesbian" (94). She gives a detailed reading of "In the Convent."

[5]"In the Convent" ("Au Couvent") has been reprinted in Kanes 220–21.

[6]An even broader thematic tradition among French novels into which *Mademoiselle Giraud* may be inscribed is the punishment of a sexually transgressive female character with death at the conclusion of the story, making possible a return to patriarchal moral order. Among such novels are some of the most famous in the French canon: Prévost's *Manon Lescaut* (1731), Rousseau's *Julie* (1761), Laclos's *Dangerous Liaisons* (1782), Flaubert's *Madame Bovary* (1857), and Zola's *Nana* (1880). *The Nun* and *The Girl with the Golden Eyes* may be included in this group as well.

[7]The history of the close relation between the popular novel and the theatrical melodrama in nineteenth-century France is complex

and fascinating. Many authors, not only Belot, worked more or less simultaneously in the two genres. See Brooks; Prendergast; Thomasseau; and Varielle. My comments here on the theatrical style of the popular novel are especially indebted to Varielle 219–24.

[8]Exact information about the demographics of the readership of the popular novel in the nineteenth century is nonexistent. A few scholars, however, have argued that in addition to the bourgeois, who were known to be consumers of novels, working classes read the popular novel as early as mid-century. See Nies; Thiesse.

Works Cited

Alexandrian, Sarane. "La double vie littéraire d'Adolphe Belot." *L'érotisme au XIXe siècle.* Ed. Alexandrian. Paris: Lattès, 1993.

———. *Histoire de la littérature érotique.* Paris: Seghers, 1989.

Brooks, Peter. *The Melodramatic Imagination.* New Haven: Yale UP, 1976.

Cantégrit, Claude. Preface. *Mademoiselle Giraud, ma femme.* By Adolphe Belot. Paris: Garnier, 1978. 5–7.

Duggan, Lisa. *Sapphic Slashers: Sex, Violence, and American Modernity.* Durham: Duke UP, 2000.

Faderman, Lillian. *Surpassing the Love of Men.* New York: Morrow, 1981.

Foster, Jeannette H. *Sex Variant Women in Literature.* Tallahassee: Naiad, 1985.

Guise, René, and Hans-Jorg Neuschäfer, eds. *Richesses du roman populaire.* Nancy: Centre de Recherches sur le Roman Populaire, 1986.

Hemmings, F. W. J. *The Life and Times of Emile Zola.* New York: Scribner's, 1977.

Kanes, Martin, ed. *L'atelier de Zola: Textes de journaux, 1865–1870.* Geneva: Droz, 1963.

Mitterand, Henri. "La publication en feuilleton de *La fortune des Rougon.*" *Mercure de France* 337 (1959): 531–36.

Nathan, Michel. *Anthologie du roman populaire, 1836–1918.* Paris: 10/18, 1985.

Nies, Fritz. "Rendre sa voix à la 'majorité silencieuse': Lecteurs et lectrices de romans populaires au XIXe siècle." Guise and Neuschäfer 147–64.

Olivier-Martin, Yves. *Histoire du roman populaire en France de 1840 à 1980*. Paris: Michel, 1980.

Prendergast, Christopher. *Balzac: Fiction and Melodrama*. London: Arnold, 1978.

Schor, Naomi. *Zola's Crowds*. Baltimore: Johns Hopkins UP, 1978.

Thiesse, Anne-Marie. "Lecteurs sans lettres." Guise and Neuschäfer 135–45.

Thomasseau, Jean-Marie. *Le mélodrame*. Paris: PUF, 1984.

Varielle, Jean-Claude. *Le roman populaire en France, 1789–1914*. Limoges: PU de Limoges; Quebec: Nuit Blanche, 1994.

Zola, Emile. *Correspondance*. Ed. B. H. Bakker, C. Becker, and Henri Mitterand. 10 vols. Montréal: PUM; Paris: Publications du Centre National de la Recherche Scientifique, 1978–95.

Selected Bibliography

Belot, Adolphe. *Les stations de l'amour*. Paris: Pauvert, 1987.

Bonnet, Marie-Jo. *Un choix sans équivoque: Recherches historiques sur les relations amoureuses entre les femmes, XVIᵉ–XXᵉ siècle.* Paris: Denoël, 1981.

Brown, Frederick. *Zola: A Life*. New York: Farrar, 1995.

DeJean, Joan. *Fictions of Sappho, 1546–1937*. Chicago: U of Chicago P, 1985.

Foucault, Michel. *Histoire de la sexualité*. 3 vols. Paris: Gallimard, 1976.

———. *The History of Sexuality*. 3 vols. Trans. Robert Hurley. New York: Vintage, 1988–90.

Hart, Lynda. *Fatal Women: Lesbian Sexuality and the Mark of Aggression*. Princeton: Princeton UP, 1994.

Ladenson, Elisabeth. *Proust's Lesbianism*. Ithaca: Cornell UP, 1999.

Marks, Elaine. "Lesbian Intertextuality." *Homosexualities and French Literature: Cultural Contexts / Critical Texts*. Ed. George Stambolian and Marks. Ithaca: Cornell UP, 1979. 353–77.

Sedgwick, Eve Kosofsky. *Between Men: English Literature and Male Homosocial Desire*. New York: Columbia UP, 1985.

Zola, Emile. *La curée*. Paris: Gallimard, 1981.

———. *La Curée*. [In English.] Trans. Alexander Teixeira de Mattos. New York: Boni, 1924.

———. *The Experimental Novel*. Trans. Belle M. Sherman. New York: Haskell, 1964.

———. *Pot-Bouille*. Paris: Presses Pocket, 1990.

———. *Pot Luck*. Trans. Brian Nelson. Oxford: Oxford UP, 1999. Trans. of *Pot-Bouille*.

———. *Le roman expérimental*. Paris: Garnier, 1971.

TRANSLATOR'S NOTE

This translation is of the 1870 E. Dentu edition of *Mademoiselle Giraud, ma femme*. The brief note to the reader that follows the preface in this edition appears to have been included in all editions of the novel. The preface by Zola first appeared in 1879 and was subsequently included in almost all editions. My translation of the preface is of the text as printed in the 1889 F. Roy edition. The only modern reprinting of *Mademoiselle Giraud* in French was in 1978 by Garnier, edited by Claude Cantégrit.

My primary goal in translating Belot's novel was to render the original tone: dynamic, vibrant, often comical (both intentionally and unintentionally) and highly theatrical. In a novel that reads like a play, much of the text is composed of dialogue.

One feature of Belot's prose proved especially challenging. He tends to write run-on sentences. To translate them in a structurally faithful way was to risk sentences in English that were at best cumbersome and at worst ungrammatical. But changing the structures too much—by breaking some of these single sentences into two or three—risked failing to communicate the rhythm of Belot's text. This quandary forced me to be more creative with punctuation than I would normally have chosen to be; the result is many more colons and semicolons than is usual and more instances of commas separating clauses than is, strictly speaking, good form in English.

To my mind, the most salient feature of the novel is that it is a true page-turner. To capture that quality and afford the reader of the translation the pleasure of galloping through the suspenseful and plot-driven narrative, I chose to keep syntax and vocabulary as simple as possible. This strategy sometimes ran the risk of creating a translation that sounded somewhat too modern for a text written in 1870. My hope was that a bit of stylistic anachronism here and there would be balanced out by the merits of a fresh, lively text. Like many translators of period works, I tried to create a text that would capture at once the period flavor and the vitality of the original.

An English translation of *Mademoiselle Giraud* was published in Chicago in 1891, by Laird and Lee. To my knowledge, there has been no other previous English translation of Belot's novel.

ADOLPHE BELOT

Mademoiselle Giraud, My Wife

PREFACE

Adolphe Belot has just published a book that has managed to capture public attention, in the midst of this time of political unrest: *Mademoiselle Giraud, My Wife*. It seems that thirty thousand copies of the novel have already been sold. For more than a year now, it is the only book that has been able to tear a large body of readers away from the ever-growing number of newspapers that may well kill off books altogether.

Such a phenomenon is worthy of scrutiny. I have just read Belot's work and now I understand its success. The masses thought it would provide fodder for their prurient curiosity. They hoped to find, in this solemn and merciless novel, the same naughty secrets found in certain cheap newspapers. Furthermore, at the same time that they were reading these vigorous and healthy pages, which their taste for scandal tried in vain to sully, they were proclaiming that the work was shameful, pretending that its title couldn't even be mentioned in front of women, virtually accusing its author of having tried to cash in on the more shameful tastes of the day.

I like clear statements. The real truth is that, even as they made the author a success by buying the book, many people were using the dirty word *immorality*, a word devoid of meaning with respect to literature. These days, when the public deigns to read one of our books, it seems to be telling us, "We are reading you, but it is only because your work is thoroughly obscene and we like spicy stories." Soon enough, success itself will become a crime, grounds for suspicion of corrupting public morals; as soon as two thousand copies of a book are sold, people will start wondering what risqué descriptions the author must have included in his novel in order to make two thousand people condescend to buy it.

Having read *Mademoiselle Giraud*, I have set as my goal to obtain absolution for Belot for his success. Someone needs to say, "Hold on! Don't lower your voice, let's talk openly about this book that you want to turn into the kind that your wives and daughters hide under their pillows. Since we still guillotine people in broad daylight, we can surely brand publicly certain vices with a red-hot iron. Don't you realize that you are foolishly and cruelly making a shameless speculator out of a moralist who has had the great courage to point out one of the scourges of the education of young girls in convents?"

I know it is considered good form to hide vice so that virtue can flourish without shame. People underestimate virtue's strength. It is precisely because virtue is virtuous that it can be exposed to hearing absolutely anything.

So let's not be hypocritical, all right? We are all very savvy these days. We are perfectly happy to whisper in one another's ears the same things we forbid our moralists to decry out loud. Belot hasn't told anyone anything he didn't already know, he hasn't compromised anyone's innocence by telling the story of a monstrous liaison between two convent-school friends. It's a story that has already made the rounds in this society of ours, rotten to the core. The author's crime is merely having disturbed the peace of mind of people who would rather whisper this story behind closed doors than see it circulate freely, with all its merciless consequences. As if to punish him for lifting the veil, people try to make him atone for his audacity by attributing to him all the scandalous intentions they themselves ascribe to his book.

No! You have misunderstood. Belot is not worthy of the kind of success you have given him. Stop hiding his book; put it on your tables, just as our fathers did with the canes with which they whipped their children. And if you have daughters, may your wife read this book before she chooses to have those dear creatures leave her and be sent off to a convent.

The story is appallingly simple. I will dare to tell it here.

5

A young man, Adrien de C., falls in love with Paule Giraud, a tall, dark-haired girl, who gives him her hand with a strange smile on her lips. Paule's friend is Berthe de B., whom she knew in the convent and with whom she has maintained a close and unwavering relationship. This Berthe, a blonde with gray eyes and red lips, had at one point made a love match, if one is to believe the rumors; then her husband left her, for reasons that were never known, leaving society to blame the husband, who never condescended to defend himself. In any case, when she learns that Adrien wants to marry her friend, Mme de B. seeks to change his mind, with an insistence, and a look on her face, that should have given the young man pause.

The wedding does take place, but Adrien cannot consummate the marriage. His wife intends to remain a virgin. Discouraging her husband's affections, she offers him instead only the friendship of a sister. At this point, Adrien begins to think that Paule is unfaithful to him. He spies on her and follows her; when he sees her furtively entering an unknown house, when he is sure he will surprise her in the arms of a lover, he finds her in the company of Mme de B., whom he forbade her to see. Nothing enlightens him; he is blind to the situation between the two women. Defeated in his struggle, he leaves, distraught and unable to figure out exactly what tragedy has befallen him. Before he can finally grasp the vile truth, he must first meet, in Nice, Berthe's husband, the man who ran away from his wife and accepted society's condemnation. The debauchery of the ancient world has swooped down on them; their wives have succumbed to the leprosy of Lesbos. Adrien, horrified, dreams of tearing Paule away from her shameful life. He persuades M. de B. to come back to France, in order to take his wife in one direction while Adrien drags his own wife in the other. But Berthe will not let go of her prey; she gets together again with her companion, and when Adrien, later, is summoned to Paule, he finds her dying of a terrible disease. There's nothing left for him to do but avenge her by helping the heavens drown Berthe, the girl with the golden eyes that Balzac glimpsed in a nightmare.

Such is the book. It's a Juvenalian satire. The only difference is that Belot's language is chaste in the extreme. He has none of the poet's crudeness. His is the cold, clear tone of a judge descending into human monstrosity and applying, as any decent man would, the eternal laws of punishment. Anyone can read this book. It's the transcript of a trial, during which all the filth of our society is laid out with such linguistic rigor that no one would think to blush.

And the moral of the story is blinding. When Adrien attempts to save, to redeem, Paule, she tells him with tears in her voice, "The convent is what ruined me, that communal life with companions of my own age. Tell mothers to keep their children by their sides and not to send them off to be indoctrinated into vice."

Now the public can give Belot's book whatever kind of success it sees fit. For me, it represents an act of decency and courage.

Th. Raquin

[Emile Zola]

NOTE TO THE READER

The brief statement in *Le Figaro* announcing the sudden interruption of the adventures of Mademoiselle Giraud gave rise to preconceived notions that the author feels compelled to try to destroy.

It is true that the subject of *Mademoiselle Giraud, My Wife* is a delicate one, but its form was rigorously attended to, in order to avoid any evil-sounding expression, any excessively vivid depiction, any indiscreet detail. The author often preferred to err through excessive obscurity, and he is convinced that if this novel were to fall into the hands of young readers, it would remain enigmatic for them.

As for those persons who are used to reading between the lines and understanding what is implied, they can't reproach us for having chosen a subject already chosen by well-respected authors, notably Balzac. They have at most the right to maintain that certain questions should always remain in the shadows and that it is dangerous to bring them into the light. The author does not agree, and so as not to repeat himself, he refers his readers to [pages 127–28] of this tome. If, after having glanced at the passage in question, they are not convinced, they will at least have to concede that this book was written in a serious fashion and that it contains useful lessons.

I

On a certain Tuesday night last February, the part of
Avenue Friedland that runs between Rue de Courcelles
and the Arc de Triomphe was extraordinarily animated. In
front of a Renaissance-style mansion, ablaze with lights,
both simple and elaborate coaches were dropping off a
constant stream of men in coats and women in capes.
They quickly crossed the wide sidewalk separating the
street from the houses; one side of an entry gate opened
in front of them, and a small black man in livery silently
pointed out the coatroom on the ground floor to the left.

A few seconds later, men in black formal dress and
women in hooded ball gowns of all colors, with masks on
their faces, climbed a staircase with a sculpted banister.
Once they had arrived in the first drawing room, the men
went to greet or shake the hand of a forty-five- or fifty-
year-old gentleman: tall, slim, distinguished, wearing a full
blond beard, a beard well known in Parisian society. At the
same time, the women went over to a young man standing at the doorway, exchanged a sign with him, murmured

11

a name, and lifted up a corner of their masks; having thus made themselves known, they slipped into a large gallery, covered with precious paintings and already full of guests.

You would have thought you were in the foyer of the Opera on the night of a ball, but the Opera the way it used to be, the one our fathers remember, from a time when people still knew how to chat, laugh, and have fun without either scandal or disturbance, when intrigue flourished, when society women were not victims of cynical brutalities, when the mob hadn't replaced the crowd, when wit hadn't been replaced by shouting matches.

Crowding around the master of the house—a fine and delicate wit, perhaps too delicate for our era, a true gentleman of letters, who carried with him in literary matters the burden of his distinguished birth and of his reverence for the eighteenth century, a La Tour portrait lost among the canvases of our realist age—were several very important figures from the political, social, and artistic spheres.

Women were in the minority in this gathering, and it would have been difficult to say to which social class they belonged.

Perhaps all the spheres of Parisian society had sent their most seductive ambassadresses: names of decent married women and grandes dames were whispered from ear to ear, but so too were those of fashionable kept women and popular actresses. At the end of the gallery, on the right, seated in front of an elegantly set table, three women from the theater, famous for their beauty, were attracting attention.

One, who was preparing for an upcoming role as a consumptive on one of our illustrious stages, was recognizable for her white and satiny shoulders, her round and sensual chin, and her incomparably fresh mouth. Another, famous for her jewels and her intermittent love for a great actor, had gone ahead and put her mask in her pocket, saying that she was hot, and looked beautiful and refined. The third had kept her mask on, but her utterly charming personality shone through in her expression, an expression so incendiary that last summer, when her house caught fire, her friends accused her of having started the fire herself.

To what sort of party had all these people been invited? Was it a ball? There was no orchestra tempting people to dance. A concert? Voices were barely silenced, laughter barely ceased, when an artist approached the piano. It was a party without a name, of an unusual type: a sort of masked reception.

A charming friend of ours made the rounds of the drawing rooms several times, exchanged many greetings and handshakes, tried to be discreet while staring at several women, and stopped several times in front of the buffet. A naval lieutenant on leave in Paris, he was not too shy to go up to the master of the house and ask if he hadn't by chance, in his insightful solicitude, set aside a little corner for the poor wretches who were incapable of going an entire evening without smoking.

"But of course, dear sir," replied Mr. X, "I set aside the entire third floor of the house. Cross the gallery, turn left, go up the stairs, and you will find, on a desk in my study, everything you need to satisfy your vices."

"The wretches will be eternally grateful for your generosity," cried Camille V., who hurried off to follow the directions he had just been given.

His vices were in good company: a dozen smokers already occupied Mr. X's study. The naval lieutenant took a cigar from a small bronze bowl on the mantel and, spying a vacant armchair, went to sit down. He had been nonchalantly stretched out for a minute, with his head resting on the back of the chair and his legs crossed, completely absorbed by the pleasure of savoring excellent Havana tobacco, when he thought he saw, through the thick cloud of smoke that obscured the room, the face of a friend.

He got up, took a few steps, looked more closely, and indeed recognized Adrien de C., one of his former classmates from Sainte-Barbe Preparatory School, his companion for two years, his neighbor in both classroom and study hall.

He couldn't be wrong: those were the same regular features, the same sweet and half-hidden expression, the same lips covered by a fine mustache. But such paleness on the formerly glowing face! And how thin he had become! There were premature wrinkles at the corners of his mouth, his hair was gray now, and a large bluish circle extended under each eye. Had only the passage of fifteen years brought about such a change and done so much damage? "Have I changed that much?" Camille V. wondered, in terror.

He turned mechanically toward the mirror above the mantel and realized, with some pleasure, after a short examination, that he had not aged the way his former classmate had.

"And yet," he told himself, "he hasn't led as rough and irregular a life as I have; he hasn't roamed all over the world, suffered from heat and cold, lived in unhealthy climates, braved storms . . ."

He stopped and then stared again: "Yes, but he may have suffered some great misfortune; emotional suffering is harder on some men than physical suffering. Who knows what kind of disappointment, what kind of sadness, what kind of anguish and despair fifteen years can bring?"

He had gradually moved closer and closer to his friend. Suddenly, Adrien de C., who was deep in thought and hadn't seen him approaching, looked up, recognized him, and held out his hands.

"Is it really you?!" he cried. "At last our paths cross again! What a stroke of luck! I was asking just recently what ever happened to you. As always, I was told that you were out globe-trotting and, as always, I was sorry to hear it. Now chance has brought us together after all these years, and I must say I'm delighted!"

They sat down next to each other and talked for a long time. They had so many happy memories to talk over, so many things to tell each other! Adrien de C. had endless questions for the naval officer: he wanted to know how he had risen through the ranks, what dangers he had braved, what hardships he had endured. He relished tales of his friend's long voyages at sea.

It seemed as if these stories provided a diversion from Adrien's thoughts, and that he was happy to live vicariously for a few moments, to lead a life other than his own.

But Camille V. had to stop eventually, at which point he turned to his long-lost friend to say, "Your turn, now you tell me something."

"Me?" Adrien cried with alarm in his voice. "Oh, no!"

"Come now! I told you all my secrets and now you won't tell me yours?"

"My life isn't worth talking about. All I've done is follow the career I trained for at school."

"And follow it brilliantly, from what I've heard. But you must have had so many adventures in all the time since we last saw each other, you must have so many stories to tell, so many things must have happened! First of all, I seem to remember having heard recently in Toulon that you were married two years ago. Are you happy, do you have any children?"

Adrien de C. lifted his head suddenly and looked at his friend with such a strange expression that Camille couldn't help crying out:

"Is that not a perfectly natural question? Have I hurt your feelings somehow?"

When Adrien didn't answer right away, the naval lieutenant took his hands in a charming burst of affection and said:

"You're suffering, you have some sort of great sorrow, don't you? Who would you confide in, if not me? Wasn't I your only friend, your brother? The fact that we haven't seen each other for so long doesn't mean that we've stopped loving each other, does it? You haven't already forgotten how wonderful it was when we saw each other again just a few minutes ago, have you? One glance was enough for us to recognize each other, after all those years, and before our hands even touched, our hearts were drawn to each other."

"Would that we had met earlier!" Adrien responded. "Perhaps you could have given me advice, perhaps you could have consoled me. Now, there's nothing more to do, and I have nothing left to say."

Fearing further questions and further pleading, he got up and led his friend to the drawing rooms on the second floor.

The rooms had taken on a different tenor since the naval officer left them. Now they were animated and gay. After supper, several masks had fallen, as if by accident, and one could see a number of pretty faces uncovered;

others were easy to make out behind the masks. Certain shoulders, understanding that they had an obligation to fulfill, shrugged off little by little the wraps that covered them and appeared nude and provocative.

The master of the house, no longer capable of resisting pressing requests, had just changed the plan for the party and permitted a few waltzes and quadrilles.

Chatter had turned into laughter, dancing had replaced gossiping. It was no longer a reception, it was a ball, all the more animated because it had started late and countless pretty legs had to make up brilliantly for their long inertia.

The two friends walked through the drawing rooms one last time, glancing at the groups of dancers, and then agreed to take their leave.

They walked down Avenue Friedland and Boulevard Haussmann and said good-bye, at five o'clock in the morning, on the Place de la Madeleine, promising to meet again at three o'clock that afternoon at the Hôtel de Bade, where Camille was staying.

The naval officer waited for his friend at the appointed hour, but the friend did not appear. He was starting to worry when a bellboy came to his room and handed him a letter that a messenger had just delivered. It was from Adrien de C., and here is what it said:

"I went to that party last night on Avenue Friedland hoping that the noise and the activity might distract me from my sadness. Such was not the case. I have been struggling for six weeks now with an all-consuming sorrow. Paris brings back memories that are simply too painful. I am going away, to where exactly I do not know, just putting one foot in front of the other. I hope that your friendship for me will allow you to forgive me for not saying good-bye in person. I was afraid you would ask me questions, that you would tear my secret from me, and at this point I just don't have the strength to tell it. But one day you'll hear it, dear friend; when I am calmer and more in control of myself, I do plan to write down my strange and exceptional story. I will send it to you, and if you think that it might be useful to someone else, I authorize you to publish it. I know you won't use my name, I trust your discretion and it won't occur to anyone to recognize me as the author. In any case, what difference would it make? I have no idea what is going to happen to me anyway! . . ."

Adrien de C. kept his promise. We are indeed publishing here the manuscript that he sent to Camille V. and that Camille saw fit to entrust to us.

II

My start in life, dear friend, would seem to indicate that I was born under a lucky star. I studied at Bonaparte Secondary School. Each year, I received several honors at the end of the year; in rhetoric, I got the grand prize. I applied to the Ecole Polytechnique and was third on the list of applicants to whom they offered admission. Two years later I entered engineering school, and I left there with my degree in hand. I was immediately entrusted with the construction of a tunnel on a new railroad line; it was a difficult job, and countless obstacles came up, but I triumphed to my great credit and the government made me a Knight of the Legion of Honor. I was barely twenty-five years old.

Shortly thereafter, I was offered a job in Egypt, to oversee some important projects; I accepted and, in ten years, made my fortune. I returned to France at that point with the intention of taking advantage of my position, of making a more pleasant life for myself, of perhaps getting married. Here my lucky star began to dim. I had scarcely spoken of my plans for marriage when my mentors and friends, and especially their wives, came forth with thousands of offers to help. There was a veritable competition to see who could marry me off. I was deluged with dinner invitations and tickets to balls and concerts. I was dragged off to the country. I was placed in the presence of all the eligible young girls in creation. These young ladies often deigned to smile at me and their mothers encouraged them to do so.

In short, I was what is called an eligible bachelor, a good catch: young, honored, rich, and not too bad looking. It was up to me to choose among the most charming and richest young women. I had only to bend down to pick them up, as Mme de F., one of our most elegant Parisians and my most ardent protectress, laughingly assured me.

Hard as it may be to believe, I hesitated to do so. I was demanding; I said, "This one is ugly; this one is so pretty it's frightening; this other one would suit me well, but her family is too big, I would look like the chief of a tribe; Mlle A. dresses like a lady of the lake; the beautiful Mlle B. has a voice that sounds like a peacock." Basically, I took pleasure in rooting out the smallest problems and I ended up trying Mme de F.'s patience.

Nonetheless, new attempts were made; my hesitations, my resistance exasperated my protectresses; they swore to themselves that they would win out over my bad faith. They no longer introduced me to individual heiresses; they introduced me to batches of heiresses; I had only to choose from the pile. In front of my blurring eyes paraded pale faces and glowing faces; small, medium, and large women; round shoulders and pointed shoulders; hair of all shades, from jet-black to light chestnut, from ash-blond to platinum blond; thin lips and sensually thick or curled lips; finally, noses of every shape and for all tastes. It was a never-ending procession, a perpetual magic lantern, a living kaleidoscope.

And what do you know! The parade annoyed me, got on my nerves. I reached the point where even the prettiest seemed ugly, the most charming seemed insufferable, and so, instead of choosing among these more or less divine creatures, I rejected them all out of hand.

"Oh! You are too particular," I was told. "Take care of your own affairs; we won't meddle anymore."

"But that's all I've ever asked for! Now, when I come into your drawing room, madame, you will no longer say, 'Look over there, on the left, on the third bench, she's pretty, isn't she? One hundred fifty thousand francs and hopes for more. And there, near the fireplace, that blonde, witty as the devil, and a millionaire for a father. And that third one, an angel, I was there at her birth, I would vouch for her as I would my own daughter. And as for this other one . . .' No, no, you give me a crick in my neck, madame; my head is not a weather vane. I have become an ordinary man again, I have the right to chat in a corner with a friend, without your eyes telling me: 'You're wasting your time, young man, you're not here to have fun; your future is at stake.' I can give in to the pleasure of a game of cards, I am free to enjoy an ice cream without your taking me by the hand to introduce me to an entire retinue of skinny girls who've just emerged into society. Ah! I can breathe, and if I get the notion again to get married, I swear, madame, that I will not let you know; you've spoiled the profession for me."

Three months went by, three months during which I swore to anyone who would listen that I would die single.

Ah! If only I had kept that vow! But let's not get ahead of the events to come.

Sitting on a cast-iron chair on the Champs-Elysées, I was philosophically smoking my cigar on a pleasant summer evening in 186-, when three people came and sat down a few feet away from me.

I cast a casual glance at my neighbors, and had no trouble realizing that I was in the presence of an upstanding family, composed of a respectable father, a middle-aged mother, and a daughter twenty to twenty-two years old. Completely absorbed by watching the crowd pass by, they hadn't exchanged a single word since they sat down, when the father said to his daughter:

"Paule, I would recommend that you get another chair, yours is wet."

"No, it's quite dry," responded somewhat curtly the one they called Paule.

"You're wrong, you'll be coughing tonight, I'm warning you."

"Well then! I'll cough."

"Come, child, be reasonable, listen to me; I'm only saying this for your own good."

The girl, instead of answering, gave the slightest shrug of her shoulders. The father was no doubt going to insist again, when his wife said, "She'll do just as she pleases: don't even try to convince her, you'll be wasting your breath."

"Well!" I thought. "It seems as if this Paule is in possession of a strong personality. The man who marries *her* will be a happy mortal. And to think that she may have been one of the infamous parade of eligible girls at one point, no doubt introduced to me as a model of all perfections! Let me see if I recognize her . . ."

I moved my chair forward, because the father's height hid most of the daughter from me.

I was dazzled.

And yet I had certainly seen my share of beautiful girls before, in the days of the parade!

This one surpassed even the most beautiful.

Ah! My poor friend, I will never forget it. As much as I try to rationalize, as much as I try to resist my memories, my mind calls her up in spite of myself, and she immediately appears.

She comes forward, indolent and supple, sensual in her every movement.

Although young, her breasts are voluptuously developed, and her hips, pronounced like those of a Spanish woman, emphasize all the more her slender and elegant waist. Her arched feet, nervous, flirtatiously shod in little boots with heels, graze the ground. She comes closer, and already my entire being shudders. Pungent and mysterious perfumes emanate from her and intoxicate me. Before she has spoken, I have already heard her voice—resonant, emphatic, almost masculine. She leans toward me, and I gaze at her.

Such voluptuousness in her big dark eyes, half veiled by long lashes and surrounded by bluish shadow! Such sensuality on her red lips, a little thick, curled back on themselves, and topped by a provocative patch of light down!

III

At the time, I wasn't thinking any of the things that I've just written about the beauty of the girl I had encountered by chance. I simply found my neighbor remarkably beautiful and couldn't help taking a certain interest in her every gesture. I must also admit that she didn't seem to notice that she was the object of my scrutiny; she didn't look at me a single time and indulged in none of those innocent flirtations that certain young girls, even some of the most virtuous, tend to indulge in.

Her mother and father were chatting while she, not paying any attention to their conversation, in a dreamy and distracted way watched the crowd go by. Her dazzling beauty continually attracted the attention of passersby both young and old; people stopped or even turned around to look at her. But she seemed indifferent to their admiration.

The only time I did see a spark of interest in her was when she watched a rather pretty young blond woman walk by. The woman's eccentric clothing had no doubt caught her eye, and Paule turned in order to continue looking at her.

"Clearly, Paule isn't enjoying herself with us," said her father, annoyed by his daughter's stubborn silence.

"I've said this before," replied her mother sadly. "Paule needs Mme de Blangy's company. She's bored whenever her friend isn't by her side, and we just aren't entertaining enough for her anymore."

This brief and typically maternal admonishment seemed to make something of an impression on my neighbor. She finally deigned to open her mouth.

"It's natural for me to enjoy being with Mme de Blangy. After all, she was my classmate for six years in the convent and she is still my friend."

"We're not criticizing your friendship for her," said her father, who seemed eager to get back in his daughter's good graces. "We're just sorry that it diminishes your affection for us."

"You're wrong, Father," replied Mlle Paule. "My affection for Mme de Blangy is completely different from the affection that I feel for you and cannot diminish it in any way."

"All the better then! Come talk to us a little. Why didn't your friend come along with us this evening?"

"She had guests coming for dinner, but she promised that she would try to meet up with us afterward."

"I'm afraid she might not be able to find us; the light is starting to fade, and if I'm not mistaken, the countess is a bit nearsighted."

"Oh, don't you worry about that! If she passes by, I'll recognize her," Paule said.

I was following every word of this conversation, having gradually inched closer to my neighbors. I was all the more curious because I happened to know Mme de Blangy.

I had met this lady several times the winter before at Mme de F.'s house (my eager would-be matchmaker!), and her beauty had made quite an impression on me.

I remember in fact that at one point, Mme de Blangy eclipsed in my mind all the eligible young girls being paraded before me; as soon as she showed up, I tended to forget (much to Mme de F.'s chagrin) all the quadrilles I had promised. Unceremoniously abandoning all notions of marriage, I would retreat into a corner to chat with the newly arrived Mme de Blangy.

As blond as her friend Paule was dark, Berthe de Blangy had a charm all her own: her big blue eyes revealed her to be both guileless and audacious; her voice was infinitely sweet; her mouth was almost exceptionally small but contained lovely teeth, set close together; her round and plump chin, with its little dimple, would have set a physiognomist dreaming. Even other women had to admire her perfectly formed shoulders, and men certainly didn't complain about the fact that her dresses were as low-cut as decency allowed.

Her quick wit, always ready with a comeback—indeed, full of clever remarks of all kinds—surprised and charmed people. Pince-nez in hand, she would descend on you all of a sudden with her imperious manner and ask you the most shameless questions, only to follow up with a remark so naive that a convent-school girl would have been ashamed to make it.

In short, she was the most seductive of women, and I was indeed so entranced at a certain point that I dared to tell her this one day. She came right up to me, stared directly at me with the help of her pince-nez, and said, "You're wasting your time, dear sir; I had a husband who was enough to make me allergic to all men; I have no desire to replace him."

Instead of saying, "I had a husband," she could have said, "I have a husband," for the count de Blangy, I was assured, was still living in some corner of France or abroad. Rich, titled, very well thought of in society, an attaché at the Ministry of Foreign Affairs, where all sang his praises, he had, two years earlier, in a drawing room of the Chaussée-d'Antin, suddenly found himself in the presence of Berthe and Paule, the two convent-school friends, the two insepa-rables, the blonde and the brunette, as they were called.

He was struck by the beauty of the two girls. He gath-ered some information about them, had himself introduced to their families, hesitated for a while between the blonde and the brunette, decided on the blonde, and married her. Six months went by, during which M. de Blangy's friends noticed a dramatic alteration in his features and a complete change in his personality. He was sad and silent, avoided so-cial gatherings, and appeared only briefly at the ministry. He went there one last time in the winter of 186–, to ask for an unlimited leave of absence and to announce that he was embarking on a journey of several years' duration.

Indeed, he left three days later, and it was never known where he was headed.

People in society had much to say about this precipitous departure and total disappearance after six months of marriage. Some people tried to explain the count's behavior by claiming that he had been cruelly disappointed in his marriage, and that he was fleeing, simply and with neither recriminations nor outcry, as a true gentleman would, a wife who was not worthy of him. But since these comments were not based on any proof, fact, or statement that M. de Blangy had let slip, they did not harm for long the respect in which the countess was held.

Moreover, if her manners were a bit eccentric, her behavior was never suspect. She received no man in an intimate fashion, and she was never seen other than in the company of her friend Paule.

Such was the woman for whom my neighbors waited and who soon appeared among the passersby.

I was the first to see her approaching, on the arm of an elderly gentleman whom she had no doubt asked to accompany her and whom she sent away as soon as she met her friends. She entered noisily into the little circle formed by my neighbors, kissed Paule on both cheeks, and sat down by her side, at some distance from the parents.

I would have loved to overhear a bit of the conversation between the two young women, but they were speaking so softly that I wasn't able to satisfy my curiosity.

A half hour later, my neighbors got up and walked down the now nearly deserted Champs-Elysées.

The countess led the way, leaning on Mlle Paule's arm. The mother and father followed them.

After they left, I too got up, headed in the direction of the traffic circle, went into the circus to watch the last acts, and then returned to my bachelor's quarters.

I slept badly that night. The memory of the beautiful Paule haunted me for a long time. Her features, so pronounced, were already as deeply engraved in my mind as they are today. Her resonant and masculine voice echoed in my still-charmed ears. I saw her big eyes, alternately bold and languorously lowered. I repeated her every word over and over to myself.

Her enthusiasm when talking about Mme de Blangy, the pleasure that suddenly was written all over her face as soon as the countess appeared, had especially struck me. A girl who understood friendship so well should, I thought, understand love beautifully. There must be hidden treasures of tenderness in her heart, passions as yet unleashed but ready to blossom.

What I had been able to surmise of her difficult personality, far from giving me pause, also delighted me. Indeed, all the girls to whom Mme de F. had introduced me were, according to her, models of all the virtues, veritable angels who had somehow wandered into human life. In perpetual contact with all these perfections, I had gotten to the point where I was crying out for some little physical or moral flaw, even some pleasant little vice; it would have been a nice change for me, but no one was ever willing to procure any such imperfection for me. Mme de F. insisted on praising her protégées to the heavens and giving them angel wings; one eventually had to agree with her. So I was thrilled at having found the longed-for imperfection in a girl, an eligible girl no doubt, and I finally fell asleep at five o'clock in the morning, telling myself that if I hadn't sworn to stay single, Paule would suit me in many ways.

The next day and the days that followed, I couldn't keep myself from thinking every minute about my pretty neighbor. I even went several times to the Champs-Elysées, hoping to see her, but she wasn't there. At the same time, almost without realizing it, I was slowly revisiting my former ideas about marriage. I admitted that I hadn't had any serious reason to abandon them. I found a thousand reasons for despising my life as a bachelor: my clothes were poorly cleaned, I was poorly served and poorly fed, my valet stole from me; in short, my house needed the discerning supervision of a woman.

My long solitude began to weigh on me, and I acknowledged that the moment had come for me to establish a household and a family for myself.

All this thinking helped me resolve, after a week of struggle and hesitation, to take the step that was clearly prescribed by the circumstances: I went one fine day to Rue Caumartin, to Mme de Blangy's house.

IV

The countess was alone in her drawing room when I was announced around three o'clock in the afternoon.

She greeted me by saying, "Well then, what have we here? So you're not dead after all!"

"Not entirely, madame; did you hear that I was?"

"No, but having completely lost sight of you, I might well have thought so."

"I thought you would be in the country this time of year, countess, and that's what prevented me from—"

"If you thought I was in the country," she said, interrupting me, "what made you think I had come back?"

"I had the pleasure of seeing you recently on the Champs-Elysées."

"On the Champs-Elysées! As a matter of fact, I did go there last week. Why didn't you come over and say hello to me?"

"It was almost dark; you probably wouldn't have recognized me."

"It's entirely possible; I have such wonderful eyesight!"

"Also," I continued, "you were sitting with several people who don't know me."

"Yes, the Giraud family, I remember; we're very close."

"I realized that from their impatience in waiting for you. Especially the girl; she had been looking for you in the crowd for some time when you finally arrived."

Mme de Blangy reached for the lorgnette hanging around her neck, aimed it in my direction, and answered, "Paule Giraud is my best friend."

"You couldn't make a better choice of friend," I replied. "Mlle Giraud is deliciously pretty."

"Isn't she, though?" said the countess rather smartly, as if happy to hear something good said about her friend.

Then, as if having thought better of her last comment: "You like brunettes now?" she asked.

"My goodness, countess! I've always appreciated beauty of all kinds."

"For that I congratulate you. But last winter, if I remember correctly, you were more particular: you seemed to believe only in blondes."

"What can I say? Blondes didn't believe in me."

"They must not have been very smart then. Are you happier with brunettes?"

"I've only met one I liked, and she doesn't even know me."

"Perhaps that counts in your favor," responded Mme de Blangy, with her usual impertinence. "And this brunette," she immediately added, "her name is no doubt Mlle Giraud?"

"But, countess . . ."

"Come now, don't try to be clever with me. Don't you think I was able to figure out why you came to see me?

You don't give a sign of life for six months, not even a card at my door. Then, suddenly, you drop into my drawing room, out of nowhere, with no warning, only to slip my friend's name into the first few words of conversation and to sing her praises. You must think me awfully dense! Don't worry, I understand: you saw Paule, you found her charming, and since you are obsessed with the idea of marriage, you've come here to ask for information about my friend. Am I right?"

"You're right."

"Good, at least you're being honest. Well then! Paule just turned twenty-two. She's very pretty, as you know; witty, I am informing you; very set in her own ideas, I am telling you because you would hear it anyway; and her family can't afford to give her any dowry, I must make known to you."

"The last detail doesn't matter to me one way or the other."

"You really are frightening."

"I've worked hard up until now," I continued, not paying any attention to the interruption, "in order to be able to marry the woman I choose, without having to take into account her fortune. I will care only about her personal qualities and the respectability of her family."

"Well, as far as Paule's personal qualities are concerned, they are charming in my opinion," said Mme de Blangy with an almost mocking smile. "On the other hand, they might not be appreciated by her husband."

"Why would you say that, madame?"

"Because men are so strange! But let's continue. The respectability of the Giraud family is very well established. Mme Giraud is an excellent woman, kind, indulgent, incapable of believing in evil, and with an extremely soft spot for her daughter. M. Giraud, head of an office in a large government agency, leaves home at nine in the morning, returns home at six for dinner, and spends his evenings at his club when he doesn't have to go back to the office. At the end of each month, he regularly brings home two-thirds of his salary to give to the two ladies to run the household, and doesn't concern himself with anything else. He's a very decent man who is incapable of seeing beyond the end of his nose."

"Meaning that there's something to be seen?"

"I'm not saying that; it's just a vulgar, but useful, figure of speech that I think describes M. Giraud's character rather well. So there you have it, as far as the family goes; do you need more information? Go ahead and ask me, I'm feeling generous today. It's raining, my nerves aren't bothering me, and I believe in friendship . . . I would almost be willing to do you a favor. In fact, I will, by giving you a piece of good advice."

"I'll gladly accept it."

"Go back as quickly as you can to Mme de F.'s, where I met you last year, and tell her: 'Madame, you must have a nice selection of marriageable girls. Please be so kind as to have them parade before me, I promise you that this time I will make up my mind.'"

"In other words, countess," I remarked, "you advise me not to consider Mlle Paule."

"I advise you simply to go back to Mme de F."

"Because Mlle Giraud is not part of her selection."

"If that's the way you want to look at it. There's my advice. Will you follow it?"

"I would like to know beforehand if it's completely disinterested."

"Sir! Are you saying that . . . ?"

"Yes, in the advice that you've just given me with a kindness for which I thank you, isn't there a bit of selfishness?"

"What do you mean by that?" Mme de Blangy cried sharply.

"Good Lord, countess!" I replied. "The feeling that I dare ascribe to you is perfectly natural. When one has an intimate friend, one is always sorry to see her get married: she doesn't belong to you the way she did in the past, you often lose the influence that you had over her, and her heart can slip away from you."

"Oh, I have no doubts about Paule; she will continue to love me."

"And she will be right to do so, madame," I replied. "That is to her credit."

"So," she began again, "far from compelling you to re-nounce your plans, everything I've been telling you for the past hour has only strengthened them?"

"I must admit that . . ." I stammered.

"I am a generous woman: going against all my usual practices, I give you an excellent piece of advice, and in-stead of following it you try to find what sort of personal motivation on my part might have dictated it."

"But . . ."

"You have made my nerves act up again, dear sir; it is only fair that I take them out on you. First of all, would you allow me to get a good look at you? Thanks to my nearsightedness, I don't think I have a very clear idea of what you look like. You flirted with me at one point, but I will admit to you now that I turned you away on princi-ple alone, which cannot possibly insult you. Today, my friend's happiness is at stake, and I no longer have the right to be so indifferent."

Not giving a thought to obtaining my consent, the countess then armed herself with her lorgnette, came right up to me, and inspected my face with it.

"The features are fine, distinguished," she said after a minute. "You are what is commonly known as a pretty boy."

Since I felt obliged to bow laughingly in order to thank her, she went on: "After having given you sufficient credit for your physical perfections, I must add that you are one of those men put on the earth to be loved very calmly, very prudently, by a good little wife, but who should give up the idea of inspiring a grand passion. Women fall violently in love only with men who are either remarkably ugly or whose beauty is pronounced and energetic. Mirabeau or Danton, those are the preferred types. You don't look like either one, so you should aim only for pretty little affections. In that sense, you are indeed the husband that would suit my friend Paule."

"What do you mean?" I asked.

"I mean what I mean. You can interpret it as you like."

"You mean, no doubt," I insisted, "that husbands and wives don't necessarily have to love each other passionately."

"I don't mean anything. Let's take another look at you, this time in terms of character. Do you promise to answer me honestly? Keep in mind that we are discussing my friend's future, and your own."

"I promise to tell nothing but the truth."

"Were you a good student in school?"

"Excellent; I always won all the honors in my class."

"So you were one of those students they call 'brains'?"

"Good Lord! Yes, madame, I admit it."

"And after you finished school, you no doubt led the life of a Parisian bachelor?"

"I didn't have the time, madame; I immediately entered the Ecole Polytechnique."

"Very good! But when you finished there?"

"I went on to graduate school in engineering."

"This is sounding better and better. And afterward?"

"I stayed in the provinces for two years, building a tunnel."

"That's very sensible. And once the tunnel was completed?"

"I left for Egypt, where I lived for ten years, busily digging canals and building railroad lines."

"So you've lived the life of a hermit."

"More or less, madame."

"Don't ever be ashamed of it. There's something to be said for hermits."

The mocking smile that had been on the lips of the countess for a moment disappeared; she became serious and said, "From the examination that I have just made you undergo, dear sir, and to which you so graciously consented, I draw the following conclusions, as my lawyer would say: You are a good young man, a decent boy, and you deserve to be happy. I thus reiterate, and this time from the bottom of my heart, my advice that you go back to Mme de F., give her the little speech we talked about, and marry as quickly as possible the least skinny of her protégées. If, at this point, you choose not to heed my advice and to go ahead with the plans that brought you here, then I wash my hands of the whole thing and will probably advise Paule to marry you. Given the fact that she needs to get married sooner or later, you are exactly the type of husband that would suit her best. Having said all that, I've spoken my piece. Good-bye and good luck; your fate is in your own hands."

V

Such was my conversation with Mme de Blangy. I have tried to make you understand all the nuances, I have recounted all the details. Unfortunately, they didn't strike me then the way they strike me now. I didn't give her advice, offered in a moment of generosity for which I should have been grateful, the importance it really had. I continued to believe that it was not disinterested and that the countess, jealous of Mlle Giraud's affection, selfishly wanted to put off as long as possible her friend's marriage.

Nonetheless, I probably would have given up my plans and forgot my pretty neighbor from the Champs-Elysées, if chance hadn't placed me once again in her path.

One evening, a week or so after my visit with Mme de Blangy, I saw Mlle Giraud at the Opera, in a box, accompanied by her mother and a gentleman of about fifty whom I recognized as a friend of my family.

The incomparable beauty of the countess's friend shone for me in a different way this time: the lights gave her skin a marvelous luster, her large dark eyes sparkled, between her reddened lips appeared dazzlingly white teeth, and her rather low-cut dress offered a glimpse of charming shoulders. Seated downstairs in a corner, lulled by the music of *Lucia*, I admired her perfections all night long.

That evening sealed my fate.

Just between us, dear friend, I deserved the epithet of "hermit" given to me by Mme de Blangy. My life, extraordinarily busy between the ages of eighteen and twenty-five, had taken me away from Parisian pleasures, and in Egypt, you know, good luck in love is rare.

I was thus thirsty to drink from certain cups, to live life after having merely vegetated, to experience strong emotions; Mlle Giraud seemed just the woman to provide them to me.

In short, as you have surely figured out by now, I was—and perhaps still am—what is called naive. Placing in the top cohort on national exams, winning the grand prize for rhetoric, and being third in one's class at the Ecole Polytechnique come at a price.

Sooner or later, one pays for such successes. Sometimes overworked intellectual faculties smother the imagination, and a bit of imagination is needed to foresee certain misfortunes and anticipate danger. In other words, be as upstanding as you like, but be aware of all human defects, in order to keep them in mind and watch out for them. Behave respectably in terms of your own actions, but don't hesitate to imagine the wildest things when it comes to judging other people. I hadn't thought enough about these excellent rules, and Mme de Blangy had read me well when, telling me good-bye, she said these words: "You are exactly the type of husband that would suit Paule."

As I told you, an old family friend of mine was escorting the Giraud ladies the evening I saw them at the Opera.

I hurried to catch up with him in the foyer during an intermission to talk to him about the woman who was already starting to have such power over me.

I had no luck there, since he could do nothing but praise Mlle Paule, whom he had known since birth and had watched grow up. According to him, she was charming and adorable; she possessed every perfection; the man who married her would be happy indeed, as she would make a wonderful wife.

I am convinced that M. d'Arnoux (that was the name of the enthusiast) believed in good faith everything he said. He was, in any case, only echoing public opinion. Thanks to our customs, we are forced to judge a girl on appearances, which are usually favorable. Only one person—and not always that one—can shed some light on her: her best friend. I had been lucky enough to be acquainted with Mlle Giraud's best friend; she had been so kind as to give me excellent advice, and I didn't follow it. I deserved my fate.

It didn't take M. d'Arnoux long to notice how attentively I was listening to what he was saying. He then guessed why, asked me about my plans for the future, and, having perhaps as much fondness for me as for Mlle Paule, kindly proposed to introduce me to her family. I made the mistake of accepting his offer. "I want to judge for myself," I told myself, "to know who is right: M.

d'Arnoux, a respectable, almost venerable, older man, or Mme de Blangy, a scatterbrained woman. If Mlle Giraud strikes me as having flaws that could threaten my peace of mind, there will still be time to renounce my plans."

Absurd logic: a man in love, as I was becoming, doesn't see flaws. If by some impossible twist they leap out at him, he glosses over them, and if there's no way to gloss over them, he turns them into virtues.

Three days after the meeting at the opera, I made my entrance into the Giraud family apartment, on the same street as Mme de Blangy's.

I won't give any details about that visit or the ones that came after. M. Giraud received me with great cordiality. His honest and open manner seemed to say, "Before receiving you in my home, I made some inquiries about you and the responses were excellent. I am delighted that you are considering my daughter, try to please her, and I will give your marriage to her my most eager consent." Mme Giraud was more reserved at first. Perhaps she didn't share her husband's hopes for me; or perhaps, in constant contact with Paule, she had borne the brunt of her daughter's personality and feared that she would make a bad impression on me.

Slowly, however, when she saw that I was falling more deeply in love with her daughter every day, and that Paule's flaws didn't seem to frighten me, the ice melted and the respectable woman developed a real affection for me.

As far as Paule was concerned, I could never accuse her of having flirted with me and led me down the primrose path to the altar. From my first visit, she was indifferent to me, an attitude she maintained the entire time I courted her. But, without being overly naive, I might well have been mistaken about her feelings for me. What seems like coldness on the part of a girl is often only reserve and shyness. So we tend to be delighted when we should be concerned, and a man with any self-regard at all expects, after the wedding, to play the role of Pygmalion to his wife's Galatea. That role seemed irresistibly appealing with respect to the person I've attempted to describe to you, and everything seemed to indicate that a mere breath would bring that admirable statue to life.

In short, six weeks after my introduction to the Giraud family, M. d'Arnoux took on the responsibility of officially asking for Mlle Paule's hand for me.

The father could not conceal his joy, the mother kissed me and cried, and the daughter, when consulted on the matter, responded that she would do whatever her family wished.

As for Mme de Blangy, whom I had seen nearly every day at the Girauds', but who had never mentioned our conversation, took advantage of a moment when we were alone, the evening of the proposal, to say to me, "You really *are* an imbecile, dear sir!"

Far from being angered by this impertinent outburst of ill humor, I laughed, because I interpreted the countess's words to mean, "I am enraged to see you marry my friend, she's going to get away from me, and I won't know what to do with my time and my affection."

The proposal officially accepted, we had only to wait the few days required for the legal formalities.

Do you realize, dear friend, the situation in which I find myself? I do not claim that it is terribly sad, and I do not ask you to pity me; but as a faithful historian, I need to inform you of all my little tribulations.

The last days before a wedding send the nervous system into a genuine state of overstimulation. There are so many worries, so many things to take care of!

A friend wakes you up to offer you his . . . condolences; a former mistress sends you four pages' worth of epigrams, she pretends to mistake your wedding for your funeral and proposes to attend, even though she hasn't been invited, the sad ceremony; merchants want to supply the basket of wedding presents for the bride; a cashmere shawl salesman comes to your house to offer you his exotic products. Women from the market bring you a bouquet of flowers, and the manager of a nanny agency (yes, dear friend, a nanny agency) wastes no time in writing you to ask that you keep him in mind when the time comes.

You also have to pressure the upholsterer who hasn't delivered the furniture for the bridal chamber yet, make the indispensable visits, order the daily bouquet and the necessary coaches, go to the tailor's and to city hall, ask the priest to please say the mass himself and to give one of those little homilies that prove to the guests that you have a certain standing in the eyes of the clergy of your parish. And eventually you have to think about going to confession, and I assure you that is no small matter when you are out of the habit.

Finally, if you're really in love with your wife, and you see the impatiently awaited day drawing near, your blood races, your heart beats faster, and at certain moments you even have a touch of fever. You certainly aren't going to find any peace and calm on the big day itself. Typically, you've slept badly because you had countless things to think about and you had to get up at the crack of dawn to tend to important details, exasperated by having to get dressed in formal clothes at an hour when elegant Parisians are still in bed. You curse your coachman who is late, you run to your mother-in-law's house, where she feels compelled to shed a few tears and where your father-in-law takes you by the collar to say, "Make her happy."

You get to the church, where the guests have been impatiently waiting for an hour, and cross paths with a funeral coming out. At the altar, you do one clumsy thing after another: you sit when you're supposed to stand; you stand when you're supposed to sit; you say yes instead of no to the priest, and vice versa; you drop the wedding ring; you choose a friend to hold up the canopy, and he tells you to go to hell. After the mass, three hundred people rush into the sacristy, a space that is ordinarily a tight fit for the dozen clergymen of the parish alone. You are jostled, squeezed, and hurried. The blood rushes to your head; you feel awful, at a moment when you had such a lovely opportunity to be a lovely boy. Finally, you exit this little corner of hell, only to be assailed by a crowd of beggars who shower you with blessings for fifty centimes apiece.

The day ends with a small family party from which it is impossible to escape, unless you were smart enough to whisk your bride away on the way out of the church. But that maneuver, which has become fashionable these days, is not always easy. A thousand things can get in the way. The evening is thus spent in the bosom of your new family, who have gathered together from the four corners of Paris and sometimes of all of France, to honor you. You have to smile at each relative, accept torrents of compliments, shake all the hands, kiss the most wrinkled faces.

You belong to everyone except your wife. Finally, the time comes to go home; you forget all the tribulations, the annoyances you've just endured, the fatigue that is overwhelming you, because happiness awaits you in your new home; you run to it, you rush toward the bridal chamber . . . Alas! it remains obstinately locked.

VI

"Well," you will probably say, "after such a full day, I can't feel sorry for your having to rest a bit. You are young and so is your wife: you are married for life and will easily make up for the night of which you've been deprived. Go, without further recriminations, go off to bed alone; it's the prudent thing to do."

Easy for you to say. Go off to bed alone, you say? Where? Do you think that I have several bedrooms and several beds in my new apartment? No, dear friend. After having pondered the question in a mature manner and read carefully the theory of the bed in *The Physiology of Marriage*, I came to agree completely with Balzac on the subject. I even impregnated myself, so to speak, with several of the ideas of the great doctor of the conjugal arts and sciences, as he calls himself. Allow me to quote you several of the ones I still remember:

"The marriage bed is a defensive weapon for the husband."

"It is only in bed that he can know every night if his wife's love is growing stronger or weaker. There is the true conjugal barometer."

"There are no more than one hundred husbands in any given European country who know enough about marriage (or life, if you will) to be able to live in rooms apart from their wives."

"Not all men are strong enough to be able to undertake living in rooms apart from their wives, whereas all men can more or less get around the difficulties that come with having only one bed."

I had espoused the opinion so clearly formulated by one of the greatest geniuses of our time, and since the only bed in my new apartment was occupied by Paule, I had to resign myself to stretch out as best I could, completely dressed, on the sofa in my living room.

I don't think I will surprise you, my friend, in telling you that I slept as badly as it is possible to sleep, in spite of the fatigue of the day. First of all, I woke up several times, if you can call it waking up, telling myself that perhaps my wife had relented and that the door was unlocked. A useless effort! The door was still locked tight. After each fruitless attempt, I would stretch out again and not be able to fall asleep. It's not that I was exaggerating the situation, but I couldn't help trying to find the causes for my dear Paule's unusual (to say the least) behavior.

"If the bolt was improperly installed," I asked myself, "could it lock itself when the door was closed? No, in that case, she would have answered when I knocked. Tired, feeling ill, she must have wanted to be alone this first night! So she had little faith in the delicacy of my feelings. I would have understood her at the slightest word, I would have withdrawn; I would have merely asked her for a pillow. She has three of them, while I . . ."

You can guess all the remarks I might have made during my long sleepless night; I'm sure you'll be grateful if I spare you the rest.

Around eight in the morning, when I heard the servants stirring in the house, I hurried to get up from my virginal couch, where I would not have been proud to be found alone, and I went into the dressing room in order to make myself look presentable.

A minute later, I rang for the maid; pretending to have just left the bridal chamber and to speak on behalf of her mistress, I gave her several orders.

Breakfast found me in the presence of Mlle Giraud. (You aren't surprised by the fact that I am still calling her by her maiden name, are you?) She came toward me with neither eagerness nor coldness, and held out her hand as you do to an old friend whom you are happy to see again.

Her morning ensemble suited her beautifully; I had never seen her fresher, more charming, more rested. No wonder.

She chatted wittily, cheerfully, like a woman who has decided to brighten up the house she's just come into, to bring it smiles and joy. You never would have guessed that she was a new bride, she was so at ease, making sensible recommendations, already taking over the reins of the household, but without arrogance, without severity, with a supreme grace. I listened to her, watched her in silence, and was truly delighted.

I was too tactful to allude to the strange way I had spent the night. I simply said, smiling, "You must have been very tired last night, my dear Paule."

"Oh, very tired," she said, "but I slept very well and now I'm well rested."

These few words seemed to contain an explanation and a promise; they satisfied me completely and managed to put me back in an excellent mood.

Around three o'clock that afternoon, Mme de Blangy was announced. She entered imperiously, as usual, kissed Paule, and held out her hand to me.

"As you can see," she said to me, "I can't do without my friend; you'll have to get used to seeing me."

"That's an easy thing to get used to," I answered, bowing.

"Oh!" added the countess. "In spite of your cordiality, I have no illusions. I will sometimes bother you a bit, but I've decided to pretend not to notice, and I have indiscreetly come over the very first day, against all rules of good social conduct, so that you will get used to my lack of manners and my impetuous visits as quickly as possible."

"You will always be welcome, countess."

"Wonderful, that's very clever of you; it's always in the best interest of a husband to treat his wife's best friend well. Don't you think?"

"Let's forget about my best interest, madame, and speak only of my pleasure."

"That's extremely gallant, and my esteem for you is growing by leaps and bounds. If you're not careful, it will become positively gigantic. By the way, are you the jealous type?"

"I really don't know. It depends."

"Would you be jealous, for example, to see Paule telling me her little wifely secrets, as she told me her girlish secrets?"

"I haven't really given that much thought, countess."

"Well, here's your chance to think about it. I am going with your wife into her room, we're going to lock the door, and I warn you that we are going to talk about you the entire time. If you can pass that first test, you've got the strength you will need."

"Let's see if I've got the strength I will need," I replied.

Since all she had been waiting for was that permission, Mme de Blangy happily took Paule by the waist, and the two young women ran away, laughing.

Far from being angry at the countess for having taken Paule away from me, I was almost thrilled about the tête-à-tête to which I had consented. A married woman can sometimes be a source of good advice for a girl, and it had occurred to me, during my sleepless night, to wonder if Paule might not need some preliminary instructions. Aside from that, I'll admit to you this most banal detail: I was dead tired and delighted to have the chance to close my eyes for a minute.

When, an hour later, I opened them again, the two friends, back in the drawing room, were chatting in front of the fireplace. They didn't notice that I was awake, and I was able to examine them at my leisure.

The contrast between their respective styles of beauty was truly alluring; each brought out the other and they thus complemented each other. Next to Mme de Blangy's blond hair and blue eyes, Paule's dark hair and eyes were all the more striking; the slight plumpness of the former made the slim waist of the latter seem even more delicate and refined. Between the two of them, they possessed all the charms possible and achieved the most complete perfection.

Moreover, I don't think they were ever prettier than at that moment. Their faces radiated with happiness, and their skin, glowing no doubt because of the flame from the hearth, had more color than an hour before, when they had left the drawing room to exchange secrets in the bedroom.

Hearing me make some movement, Mme de Blangy turned around and said to me: "Did you at least sleep well?"

"But . . ." I answered, a little embarrassed.

"Come now, admit it, we're not angry at you, on the contrary. We were able to take our time chatting," she added, smiling and sneaking a glance at Paule. "Now I'll leave you two alone; I don't want my name to be cursed any more than it already is. But I'll see you soon."

No one came that evening to disturb my tête-à-tête with Paule. She was as charming as she had been that morning at breakfast. She chatted about a thousand things, she touched on several topics with a wit, an accuracy of perspective, often even a profundity, that genuinely surprised me.

I had thought I was marrying a young girl whose eyes I would have to open, and instead I was in the presence of a grown woman: witty, caustic, quick with a comeback, with a bit of a philosophical side and an imagination that was perhaps a bit licentious.

"But, my dear friend," I asked, "where in the world did you learn all this?"

"I didn't learn anything," she said, smiling. "I figured it all out."

"You must have quite an imagination."

"Well, yes, I do have lots of imagination; too much, even, which is unfortunate for me and perhaps even for you."

"When imagination is well directed, it's not a bad thing."

"Yes, but it must be well directed," Paule added, with a sigh.

"Why did you wait until today to reveal all your delicious qualities to me?"

"Because," she said, "I am not a flirt. I had advised you not to marry me, and it wouldn't have been right for me to put myself in a flattering light. You didn't listen to me, you went headlong into the danger; the damage is done, and I'm trying to reveal my qualities, as you say, in order to make myself appealing at least . . . intellectually."

At the time, I didn't notice that last word, which was spoken very shrewdly and deliberately. The entire conversation, in fact, should have raised questions for me; but try asking yourself questions at ten at night, the day after your wedding, next to a woman as beautiful as Paule, when the marriage has yet to be consummated!

Soon I was no longer even paying attention to what she was saying; my mind was occupied only by watching her, admiring her; losing my head, I took her in my arms.

She broke away gently and calmly, smiled her prettiest smile, rang for her maid, and left the drawing room.

A quarter of an hour later, when I saw the maid leave her room, it was my turn to head over to the blessed threshold that I hadn't crossed the night before.

Sure that she was waiting for me, I didn't even knock, I simply turned the knob.

VII

The door didn't open.

Like the night before, it was bolted.

So I knocked.

No answer.

I knocked more insistently.

Same result.

I spoke, I called out, I begged.

All in vain.

Can't you just see me, dear friend, asking, as if for a favor, to be allowed to enter my own bedroom? Because it *was* my bedroom; I had no other, and aside from my desire, it was only fair that I demand to sleep in a real bed.

My nerves were so overstimulated that I was about to abandon my usually calm and peaceful character and knock on the door so violently that, weary of the battle, she would have to let me in.

Fear of ridicule stopped me; I didn't want to let my servants in on the secret of my conjugal misfortune. I just pushed silently, with my entire weight, against the door, in the hope that it would give way.

A wasted effort. I didn't hear even the slightest creak; the construction of my apartment was excellent, and I could congratulate myself all too heartily for having such a good landlord.

What else can I say? That second night went by just as pleasantly as the first. The only difference is that, dead tired, I did manage to sleep fairly well.

I woke up calmer than I could have hoped to be, less angry at my wife, more inclined to excuse her. Having thought as objectively as possible about our conversation the night before, and in spite of certain details that had struck me, I thought I could draw the conclusion that Paule, far from being an ingenue ignorant of her duties, had on the contrary the most decided opinions about marriage. She no doubt thought that a husband had to go to some trouble in order to deserve his wife and that he should show his tact by pretending to forget that he had rights. For the good of our love, she wanted to make me desire her and to belong to me as a lover before becoming my wife. In short, she thought that there was something unfair and illogical in requiring that on a certain day, the minute they came out of city hall, a girl should throw herself into the arms of a man she barely knew, and she had resolved to be an exception to that barbaric custom.

There you have, my dear friend, the rationales that I came up with to explain Paule's behavior. I told myself only that she should have at least given me a hint of her way of looking at things; I would have arranged our apartment completely differently and would have acquired a second bed, given the prospect of my prolonged bachelorhood. Perhaps she was also not entirely aware of the way I was spending my nights and it was a good idea to give her some notion of that drawing-room couch, quite narrow and not very well padded, that had become my conjugal, or nonconjugal, bed for the past two days.

"The sight of that couch will touch her," I told myself, "and will probably move her to shorten my probationary period."

After breakfast, which brought us together once again, and during which we conducted ourselves, as we had the morning before, in a charming manner, I offered her my arm and proposed a little stroll through her kingdom. She accepted with impeccable grace, and we went into the dressing room, where I tried to bring to her attention the fact that there were only chairs.

She responded simply, as a good housewife would, as an economical wife would, "This furniture is enough for the moment."

Leaving the dressing room, we went into a little summer boudoir adjacent to the drawing room. There, I pointed out one of those round sofas with the tufted backs that are placed in the middle of a room and on which several people can sit with their backs to one another, and I said, "It's pretty, it's fashionable, but it would be rather uncomfortable to sleep on."

"Yes," she said, with a clever smile, "one would have to sleep bent in a circle, that would be bothersome."

At that point, I had her enter the study that I had set aside for myself, and, picking the conversation up where we had left it: "Here," I said, "it wouldn't even be possible for me to sleep in a circle; I have neither a couch nor a sofa."

"Why not?" she asked.

"Because I didn't think I would spend much time in this room; I paid particular attention to the rooms in which we were going to live together."

"You were wrong," she said. "A married man's study should be comfortable and elegant. You will receive tradesmen, various other people, and even friends in this room, which will give them an idea of the rest of the apartment. I would recommend one of those pieces of furniture that I've seen in some of the upholsterers' shops, the kind that serve as a sofa in the daytime and a full bed at night."

I looked at her; she didn't lower her eyes.

"I will follow your advice, dear Paule," I told her. "This very day I will go out and buy one of those pieces of furniture you're talking about, because, you see, I've really needed it. Where do you think I've been sleeping for the past few days?"

"I assumed," she replied, unaffected by my blunt question, "that you went off into this room. I just thought it was more intelligently furnished."

That sentence exasperated me, and I shot back rather sharply, "So you plan to continue to lock yourself in your room every night?"

"Instead of interrogating me about my plans," she said in a very sweet voice and taking my arm again to go back into the drawing room, "it would be nicer for you to try to figure out yourself what they are."

This last sentence justified the hypothesis I had come up with that morning. I was dealing not with an ingenue, not with a schoolgirl, but with a marvelously experienced young woman.

Where had she acquired this experience, this knowledge of life, this flirtatiousness that consisted of leaving my desire in suspense? Was it her mother who had told her, "If you want to make sure that he'll love you for a long time, learn how to make him wait for you. Usually, it's the ease of marital relations that kills the love in a marriage; for the sake of her own happiness, a married woman is allowed to behave in her marriage like a shrewd mistress"?

No. Paule's mother was too respectable a woman, too natural, to have given that kind of advice. She had surely respected all the rules of marriage and fulfilled, without argument or rationalization, all its duties and responsibilities. It could only have been Mme de Blangy who, wanting

Paule to take advantage of her own experience as a married woman, gave her advice on how to behave.

Well, dear friend, if you can believe this, I was not irritated at that point by the influence she had had over my wife. My esteem for the countess, shared by all society, meant that I was unperturbed, and the naïveté that you know me to possess didn't allow me to admit that a well-bred, intelligent woman like Mme de Blangy could have any reason to besmirch with pernicious advice the purity of a young girl.

Then too, I must admit, the knowledge of life that I had discovered in Paule, her resistance to my desire, far from scaring me off, had a certain attraction for me. Complete innocence, you know, is generally attractive only to the corrupt or to old men. Men who, like me, haven't yet lived, are more likely to be drawn in by certain tricks of skillful seduction. They are not put off by finding a bit of knowledge or savoir faire in a woman, and if they happen to start considering marriage, you'll often find them rather predisposed to the idea of marrying a widow.

Thus, surprisingly, I was coming around little by little to the point of congratulating myself on having found in Paule both the incontestable advantages of a young girl and a certain precocious experience due to intelligent advice or a special intuition about life.

The role of suitor, assigned to a husband, also has something original about it and fed my imagination (which, I admit, had been somewhat dormant up to that point). I think that if I had ended up with an ordinary girl, I would have made, in keeping with my calm temperament and a certain apathy that comes naturally to me, the most banal and bourgeois of husbands.

With Paule, on the contrary, my entire being was coming alive, and I was gradually leaving behind the sensual lethargy brought about in me by the excessive work I had been doing since childhood. The state of having my intellect always overstimulated and my mind always occupied with excessively abstract studies hadn't allowed me to take my heart into account; it was beating for perhaps the first time, and I was delighted to feel it beating.

I was going to live after all and to make this charming dream come true: being in love with my wife, having a legitimate mistress, uniting fantasy and reality, and substituting a worthy and beautiful passion for a love that, had Paule not taken care of things, would have degenerated into a calm, quiet habit with no spice at all.

So you won't be surprised to see that I changed, rather happily, my study into a bedroom. I set it up as best I could in order to live out the probation that had been imposed on me. I was, however, determined to use all the means of seduction Nature might have given me to shorten that trial period.

VIII

Two weeks went by, during which I was remarkably patient, discreet, and sensitive. I made no demands, I asked no questions, I didn't even utter any direct pleas. Seeing me so reserved and so platonic in my relations with Paule, you would have thought we were still waiting to be married, that we had yet to stand up in front of either the mayor or our parish priest.

I courted my wife as assiduously as possible, but made no allusions to the kind of hopes to which you, dear friend, must admit I was well entitled. Her reserve equaled mine, by the way: while it is true that I had made it my duty not to ask for anything, it is also true that she was in no hurry to offer anything. I was therefore no better off; on the contrary, it seemed to me at certain times that I was losing a bit of ground. So I told myself one morning, in my bachelor's bed, that since discretion wasn't working, it was perhaps time to try another approach.

If by any chance, my dear friend, you are surprised to see my patience wear thin so quickly, I will ask you to put yourself for a moment in my place. Don't worry, I won't leave you there very long: you've never done me any harm and I have no reason to take revenge on you.

So imagine yourself beside an adorable woman, seductive in every way, more desirable than words can say; you are in constant contact with her all day long: she charms you, intoxicates you, drives you mad, and when evening comes . . . you know the rest. Well then! How does that make you feel?

This is not a unique situation, you will tell me: everyone has found himself in more or less comparable circumstances; you court a woman for weeks, often for months, without receiving from her, for one reason or another, a direct reward. I agree with you. But the woman you are courting isn't your wife, in fact she is often someone else's, so there are many reasons for her to put off the moment of her downfall. As she stands on the brink, a thousand terrors and scruples of all kinds might hold her back; if her hesitation and resistance are torture for you, at least you know what they are and are even inclined to understand them.

But in the case we are discussing, where, I ask you, do you see good reasons to explain such a long resistance? Where are the fears, the terrors, the scruples? In short, where is the danger?

I don't know why I am trying to convince you; you were already on my side, I'm sure, even before hearing me, and if I surprise you, it is by my constant patience, which you are perhaps already calling weakness or foolishness.

Well, as of the sixteenth day of my probation, I stopped being patient, and in fact I was no longer able to be. Subjected to a constant irritation, my character had turned sour; I, who had managed for a long time to imagine that I had no nerves, was now prey to a host of the most acute nervous pains.

This unhealthy state could not go on. Since it was clear that my desires were not going to be anticipated, I decided to articulate them.

"Already!" she said, smiling.

Ah! In the state I was in, it wouldn't have taken much for me to strangle her for that word. "Already"? Didn't this woman understand anything? She obviously had neither emotions nor desires! I had thought I was marrying a woman, and instead I had made a bad match with a statue.

I restrained myself and tried to inspire some pity in her. I described for her with great eloquence the love she had inspired in my heart, I spoke to her of my emotional pain and of the physical malaise that had taken hold of me, and of which she was the cause. I begged her to have mercy on me, because I had no strength left.

She listened to me attentively, and seemed moved by what she had heard, but when I begged her to say something in response, she remained silent.

Ah, dear friend! Certain silences make one suffer horribly!

"Please speak," I cried. "Say whatever you want, but speak, I beg you."

"I have nothing to say," she answered.

"Explain your resistance, your hesitation. I promise to approve of all your reasons, but give me one, just one, please!"

She didn't answer.

At that point, furious, I brusquely got up from the sofa where I had been sitting next to her and I went to get my hat to go out. I was so exasperated by this obstinate silence, my entire nervous system was so irritated, that I was afraid of being led to some extreme behavior toward her.

Yes, an all too strong word is so quickly said, an all too brusque gesture slips out so easily, and women know only too well how to take advantage of those flashes of anger! They don't tell themselves that they are the cause, that they pushed you to the breaking point, that they were the ones who were wrong in the first place. They forget on purpose the bitter words that made us angry, and their calculated silences, and the thousand knives that they stuck in our hearts; they remember only the last words that slipped out of our mouths, the excessively meaning-ful gesture that we let ourselves make, and they turn those things into terrible weapons to be used against us.

"You are a brute!" they cry. "It's all over between us!"

I didn't want to expose myself, as I'm sure you can un-derstand, to the possibility of my wife's saying, "It's all over," when in fact nothing had begun, so I left, fearing that I would be able to restrain myself no longer.

But having taken a few steps toward the door, I sud-denly turned.

"Listen," I began again. "If you don't want to answer the questions I just asked you, fine! Let's not talk about it anymore. I only ask you one thing: to tell me when the ordeal you are putting me through will end, and I give you my word of honor to wait for that moment without complaining, no matter how far away it may be. But set a date for me, don't leave me hanging in midair; the uncer-tainty I am living with is killing me! Take pity on me; I've never done you any harm . . . I love you, I desire you ardently! Do you think that's wrong? Is it a crime for which I should be punished? Come on, be kind, let yourself give in to my pleading, to my tears, yes, my tears. See, I'm crying, I can't help it, that's how much I'm suffering!"

At that point, perhaps on the verge of letting herself be moved, she gently removed my hands, which I was trying to wrap around her, got up, and, nailing me in place with a look that I thought contained a threat—a threat that made me tremble—went into her room.

At the same moment, I heard a noise that I knew well: that of the bolt slipping into place.

Here you will stop me, won't you, dear friend, to cry out, "But why don't you just remove the bolt that is causing you so much trouble, you poor wretch? Aren't you in your own home?"

Rest assured, the thought occurred to me. I had thought more than once about exercising my authority. I realized that my pleadings, my solicitations, and my tears not only were not serving me well, they must have been damaging Paule's image of me. Women typically don't like a man who humiliates himself and begs. Supplications only move them when in line with their own secret desires. They will perhaps give themselves out of kindness, but they'll never love out of charity. Begging is forbidden in the realm of love.

I needed to take a strong stance, or else lose all stature in Paule's mind.

One evening, after dinner, she proposed that I accompany her to see Mme de Blangy, whom she hadn't seen for two days. I said yes, but upon arriving at the countess's door, pretended to have a sudden migraine that made me need some air, and I let my wife go up alone to see her friend, promising to come back for her.

I had scarcely left her side before I quickly returned to my apartment: I went into Paule's room and removed all the screws of the hateful bolt one by one, using an instrument I had procured that day. I broke off the tips of each of the screws and kept the heads, which I put back in their holes, giving the appearance of having screwed them in properly.

Paule couldn't possibly figure out my trick: the bolt was still solid enough to be put into place from the inside, but the heads of the screws, which were no longer held in place by their usual shafts, would fall out at the least pressure placed on the door from the outside.

When I joined my wife an hour later, I found her in the countess's boudoir, half reclining on a sofa, beside her friend.

Although my arrival had been expected, I had the impression that it disturbed these ladies. I have since thought that they were confiding in each other; Paule's eyes were wet and tired as if she had been crying, and I noticed more animation on the countess's face.

Accompanying my wife home, and then back in our drawing room, before taking leave of her, I will let you guess if I renewed my pleading of the previous days. I would have been so happy not to have to employ such extreme measures, and to let her remain forever ignorant of the little bit of locksmithing in which I had just engaged!

She was colder, drier, more discouraging than ever.

If she had given me a single kind word, looked at me with just a bit of tenderness, made me some tacit promise for even a distant future, I would certainly have renounced my plan.

Nothing: not a word, not a gesture, not a look. She seemed, that evening, not even to be aware that I was talking to her, not even to realize that I existed; never had I seen her so distracted, so detached from me.

I couldn't waver. I told her good-bye; she retired to her room. I let an hour go by so that she would have time to undress and fall asleep. Then, trembling, feverish, pale as a criminal, I headed toward the door to her bedroom.

Just as I had planned, the bolt yielded and the door opened noiselessly.

IX

So I entered.

Can you imagine my astonishment when I saw my wife, dressed as she had been an hour before, reading by the fireside?

She nonchalantly turned around at the noise I made and said to me, completely calmly, "I was waiting for you."

I managed to fight back my emotion, and leaning on the mantel across from Paule, said in return, "Why were you waiting for me?"

"Because when I went to push the bolt of my door earlier, it fell at my feet, and I figured out your plan. It was you who performed that little bit of handiwork, just like a thief or a lover, wasn't it?"

"Or a husband," I added. "Although husbands are rarely forced to go to such drastic lengths. Yes, it was me."

"So you admit it?"

"I admit it," I said firmly. "My role in this marriage is ridiculous and I have decided not to play it anymore."

"What were you hoping would happen, if I hadn't figured out your strategy?"

"I was hoping to prove my love to you."

"By using violence on me," she said with a disdainful smile.

"Yes, by using violence on you, if you forced me to; but God is my witness that I had tried everything possible to touch your heart before I considered going to that extreme. But neither my patience nor my sensitivity nor my pleas were able to move you."

"Rest assured that I am less moved than ever at this point."

"You couldn't be any less moved; you were never moved at all."

"You don't know that. In any case, your behavior this evening has outraged me, and I am telling you once and for all that from now on, all your attempts will be in vain."

"Ah! So it's my behavior this evening that determined that decision?"

"Yes."

"That's not true!" I suddenly cried, violently. "Because up until today you had nothing whatsoever to reproach me for, I showered you with care, with attention, with kind gestures, and you never took pity on me! What is the reason behind your hardness? I want to know."

She remained silent.

Then, in a state of nervous overstimulation that is impossible to describe, I grabbed her wrists, squeezed them hard, made her get up, and said to her, "Answer, I demand it."

"You're hurting me," she cried.

"Answer, I want you to answer me."

"No, I won't answer you! Violence has never got the better of me. You don't know me very well yet! Well, start learning something about me right now: it will serve you well in the future. I will get what I want, so there! And what I don't want to happen will never happen. All your strength will just use itself up against the force of my will and you will exhaust yourself in a useless struggle."

While she was talking to me so harshly, each one of her words stabbing me directly in the heart, would you believe, dear friend, that I couldn't help looking at her and admiring her?

Her long hair had come undone and was hanging down around her shoulders; I saw her chest heaving under the blouse that barely covered it; her eyes had a fire that I had never seen in them before; and behind her lips, more sensual than ever, I saw lovely teeth that were chattering with anger.

"Oh, how beautiful you are!" I cried.

And, forgetting everything that she had just said, bringing both her hands together in my left hand and holding them tight, I tried with my right hand to bring her head to my lips.

She struggled with such energy, and unleashed such force to extract herself from my embrace, that she soon escaped from my arms and I fell back, broken, on the chair where she had been sitting earlier.

At that point, insulting me in my defeat, she crossed her arms and said, "Do you still believe you can get the better of me by using violence?"

"So you really hate me!" I cried, desperate and with tears in my voice.

As happens in most nervous fits, tenderness followed anger.

This strange girl, touched perhaps by my pain, softened no doubt as I was after the struggle she had just put up, got a pillow, pulled it up to my chair, sat down, and said, "No, I don't hate you."

I looked at her; her eyes didn't have their usual expression, they were tender and kind.

"So," I asked her, "if you don't hate me, why do you make me suffer like this?"

"Don't ask me questions about that," she said gently. "I assure you that I can't answer them. But I swear to you that, far from hating you, I have a real fondness for you: I appreciate all your good points, I was touched by all your kind gestures, and to be frank, I will admit that I am not angry anymore either about your plan for this evening or your outburst a few minutes ago. Believe me, I am too smart not to understand and excuse them."

"Why," I said to her, "haven't you ever spoken to me before so gently and reasonably?"

"I was afraid of seeing you make a mistake about the nature of the feelings I have for you and of encouraging a love that I wouldn't be able to return."

"Those last words, my dear Paule, are out of line with what you were saying just before. If you do see those qualities in me, if you have real fondness for me, I can hope . . ."

"No, no," she said, suddenly interrupting me. "You can't hope anything, and that's precisely why I hesitated to open my heart to you. I was afraid you would reason the way you just did."

"You must admit that it is rather logical."

"Very logical, I agree. Otherwise, I wouldn't have feared it."

"I don't understand you."

She remained silent.

"Come now," I said, because I wanted to take advantage of the way she seemed to be seeing things, "have faith in my deep affection. I am not speaking to you as a husband (since I am not really a husband anyway!), I am speaking to you as a friend who will be completely indulgent. Perhaps you have in your heart the kind of love that young girls have, for a cousin maybe, and that takes on an exaggerated importance. Well, far from holding it against you, I will treat you like a sick child, I will surround you with care and wait for your recovery."

"No," she said, "that's not it."

"Well then, I am trying to think . . ."

"You will never guess, and it's better for your sake that you don't. Just tell yourself, 'That's the way it is,' and try to make the best of it."

"Making the best of it, my dear friend, is impossible; I am your husband, in the eyes of the law at least, even if not in actual fact."

"This marriage wasn't my doing; you were the one who wanted to contract it at all costs. Remember how it all took place: you met me for the first time, one evening, on the Champs-Elysées; did I turn my head toward you, could you have accused me of even a hint of flirtatiousness? No. You went to Mme de Blangy's house, you told her about me and your plans: what did she say? 'Paule is not right for you, give up on her.' Nonetheless, you had yourself introduced into my home, my father liked you, my mother liked you, how could I block you at the door of a home that didn't belong to me? I had to settle for treating you with a coldness that I didn't even feel, since— as I have told you—I liked you from the start. Three weeks went by, and you were bold enough to ask for my hand. My entire family tried to persuade me that you were right for me in every way, and I was convinced of it myself. I nonetheless resisted, and my father, who had already seen me turn down three proposals without giving a single good reason, started to get angry and threaten me with the convent. The convent! Can you picture me, at twenty years old, going back to the convent? I who have no religious beliefs? I was afraid and ended up telling my father, 'Thy will be done!' But to you I said, 'Give up your plans; I am not in a position to turn you down, but take back your offer. You deserve to be happy, and I won't be able to make you happy.' Instead of considering yourself warned, you completely disregarded these words, you continued to take me for a child who knew nothing about life. With typical male smugness, you had no doubts about your ability to make yourself loved, and you married me. Come now, I ask you: is it my fault, and can you blame me for what is happening to you now?"

"So," I replied after a moment of silence, "for having loved you to the point of being deaf to all warnings, I am condemned in perpetuity to the most hideous of tortures: that of Tantalus."

She took my hand (I didn't have the heart to take it back) and said, "This torture won't be as painful as you think. I will be able to make things easier for you by my devotion and kind affection. Even if I don't love you the way you'd like to be loved, at least I will never love anyone else, I swear to you, because you are the only man who could have appealed to me. You will never have to complain of any flirtatiousness on my part with you, or with any of the friends you may introduce me to. My life will be lived, if you wish, in the company of my mother, you, and Mme de Blangy. Society will consider you the happiest and most beloved husband, seeing how much I surround you with kindnesses and care. In short, I will be for you the best possible sister."

I thought for a long time in silence about everything she had just said. I tried to imagine objectively the situation that had been proposed to me and to appreciate it. But suddenly my blood began to boil, my very flesh rejected the idea; rising up, I cried, "No, I will not accept your proposal. I love you passionately, deliriously, and I cannot consent to live by your side like a brother. I married you so that you would be my wife, and that is what you must be."

"Ah," she responded, "I was told that all men were egotistical and materialistic. You're obviously no better than the rest. Well then, I repeat, whether you accept what I am proposing or not, you cannot have me. I have spoken, and I am asking you to leave me now. I am exhausted and need rest. In spite of your pretensions of being a husband, you do not, at least I imagine, have any desire to be a tyrant."

X

She was wrong. I did become a tyrant.

What did I have to lose? Had she left me any hope at all? Could I believe that in time I would triumph over her resistance, that I would succeed in touching her heart? No, she had made herself as clear as possible on that question, and it would have been foolish for me to harbor any illusions. I was condemned without appeal, without the possibility of reprieve, to a life sentence of celibacy.

I exercised my tyranny, by the way, without conviction, without prejudice, with periods of cease-fire and sudden reemergences of gentleness and indulgence. It was an intermittent tyranny.

Oh, my dear friend, don't reproach me for my weakness, my lack of vigor; it is so hard to maintain constant severity toward someone one loves!

My first act of authority was to see to the question of the bolt. "Wasted effort," you will tell me, "the little locksmithing job you undertook that day got you nowhere! It wasn't your wife's door you needed to unbolt, it was her heart." You are perfectly right. But, unable to vanquish moral resistance, I took pleasure in overcoming material obstacles. I would no longer put up with barricades in my house, and I intended to enter, when I felt like it, the only bedroom in my apartment. So I lost no time in gathering up from the carpet the little instrument of my torture and putting it in my pocket.

Oddly enough, that same day, without my having seen any workmen come into the house, I saw a new bolt, the kind they call a security bolt, installed in the place of the old one. Who had put it there? My wife, obviously. Without saying a word, I armed myself with my screwdriver and undid what had just been done. The next day, a new bolt appeared. It suffered the same fate as the first two; I was becoming a collector. My wife didn't give up until the seventh bolt; she had no doubt exhausted the inventory of the neighborhood hardware store.

Fortunately, these little operations took place only between us, far from the indiscreet eyes of the servants. They continued to think of us as the happiest couple on earth, such effort did Paule put into smothering me with attention in front of them. There was never so much as a word or a gesture that could have led them to suspect the kind of domestic war that was going on between us. I am pleased to offer this homage to Mlle Giraud; it is the only one.

Had she resorted to some ruse for replacing the seventh bolt? Had she found an original way of barricading herself and keeping herself safe from inopportune visits in the night? For a long time, I had no idea. The memory of my first campaign gave me pause; I hesitated to expose myself to a new defeat and I sought refuge under my tent, like a hunter who has been discouraged by several failed excursions and stays home, for fear of coming back empty-handed again.

This bout of timidity, of pride, of dignity, of cowardice—call it whatever you like, I think there was a bit of each of those things—could not last, however.

Inevitably, I decided (as would anyone in my position) not to resign myself to my sad fate without pitching some sort of definitive battle. The day of my defeat, I had had to fight an enemy already on guard. The bolt that fell on the carpet had announced my imminent arrival, as a detonation on the ramparts announces a coming assault to those under siege. Paule had immediately armed herself from head to toe, she had lined up her artillery, and as soon as I committed the imprudence of appearing, she opened fire without restraint, whereupon I fell, wounded by her shots. This time, it was a matter of surprising the enemy, at night, while she was asleep, when she had laid down her weapons and all her armor.

I was determined to show her no mercy; not to let myself be moved by her cries, her threats, or her pleas; to be resolute and forceful, come what may; and to walk away with one of those victories so brilliant that the winner is absolved by history of the ruses of war he had to employ in order to achieve it.

It was not without a certain amount of emotion that I awaited the hour I had set for this great battle; I knew it was to have a crucial importance. When two adversaries do battle, evenly matched, on a battlefield, in full sunlight, the loser doesn't feel humiliated; he can send a new challenge the very next day, and it must be accepted. But if you attack, under cover of night, an unaware and unarmed enemy, you must either win or give up forever on a struggle that has become impossible.

I thus overlooked nothing to ensure myself a brilliant triumph; I took my time and was even so clever as to try to figure out the tactic that my adversary would use to resist me, the type of defense that she would envisage, the tricks she would deploy against mine.

My wife, that day, had gone back to her room around eleven o'clock; I followed her example and went into my study. I waited for a long time until all the noises of the house had ceased and all the lights had been turned off; then, around one o'clock, I walked quietly across the drawing room and entered the marriage chamber, not making the slightest sound. The door made no noise as it shut. A night-light hanging from the ceiling gave off a soft and mysterious light all around me. I looked over at the bed.

Paule was asleep. Her face was turned toward me. One of her arms, bare, gracefully rounded, rested on the pillow above her head. Under a sheet that failed to cover her completely, one could see the outline of a beautiful body. Let us not go any further with this: in my elegant state of undress, standing in the middle of the room, exposed to all manner of head colds, it was not the right moment for me to contemplate my wife sensually stretched out on my terrain. Didn't I have to conquer that terrain as quickly as possible and establish myself as its master before the usurper woke up?

I made up my mind to go ahead and charge. This was no small feat: the bed was one of those good old-fashioned beds, raised up like our fathers liked them and into which it is impossible to simply slip.

I had to climb up, there was no question about it. But my mind was made up, I acknowledged no obstacles. All of a sudden, at the point where my right leg had already cleared the wooden frame of the bed and was searching for a resting place on the bedsprings and my left leg was getting ready to join it, thus at the moment when I was to some extent suspended in midair, I heard a burst of laughter so loud that I lost my balance and fell, feet first, to the carpet.

Paule hadn't made the least little movement: her arm was still bent over her head and her legs were gracefully crossed, but her wide-open eyes were locked onto me, and she was laughing—laughing!

At that point I took a flying leap and threw myself onto the bed. In a single jump, I found myself standing at the foot of the bed.

Can you see me, dear friend, in this pose and in an outfit that you can surely imagine, tall as I am, my face half hidden in the bed curtains? You find me rather ridiculous, don't you? And to think that I still had to travel the entire distance from the foot to the head of the bed.

I undertook the voyage.

Paule was still laughing. Finally, I bent down, lifted the blanket, pulled it over on me and stretched out my entire body. Oh, what a bed! How big it was! I was able to take my place in it without disturbing Paule at all. How soft it was, how well I had chosen it!

Paule was no longer laughing, she was looking at me. I was looking at her too, without daring to budge from my spot. Was I not the master of the situation, was this not a sure victory?

As a matter of fact, no, it was not. I was prepared for anything, except my wife's stubborn silence, her glacial impassivity. I had expected to face an enemy who would complain, insult me, fight me off; I was ready for a struggle and I would have won it.

But those big eyes staring at me with such fixed obstinacy, those lips resolutely pursed, that insensitive, inert, somehow inanimate body, transformed me into ice. All my beautiful resolutions evaporated into thin air.

Oh, she knew what she was doing, all right, someone had told her just how to act with me. She had been told, "The more in love a man is, the easier it is to intimidate him; the more tense his nerves are, the more easily they will relax at the slightest nervous stimulation.

"Excessive emotion can turn an athlete into a child. If he forbids you to bolt your door, obey him; let him come into the room that he doesn't want to surrender to you, rest assured that you have nothing to fear from him. He himself will acknowledge the futility of his clandestine visits, he will blush at his own defeat and won't risk playing such a ridiculous role with you again."

She who had dared tell Paule such things had been right. She had complete knowledge of the defects of our poor human nature, its deficiencies and its vulnerability to discouragement.

After that, I no longer dared enter my wife's bedroom and, oddly enough, no longer dared complain. Wasn't her door left wide open to me? Had she been shocked by my inopportune visit? No. The only thing I could reproach her for was the coldness of her welcome, but I should have overcome that coldness and had not been able to. I was truly desperate. I had no more hope, no more resources.

I had wondered earlier if I shouldn't confide my sorrow to Mme Giraud, if it wouldn't be appropriate for me to say, "When you gave me your daughter, you didn't intend for us to live separately, but that is what we are doing. Use your influence on her to make her understand that marriage is not exactly a rest cure."

But what would have happened? Mme Giraud would have called in her daughter, who would have responded (if she deigned to respond at all, which was not guaranteed), "My husband is a slanderer; due to excessive feelings of prudishness, I have locked my door to him a few times, but I won't do it anymore. Nothing prevents him from coming in, and he does come in. If he's not happy there, it is his fault, not mine, and I am the one who should be complaining about him."

The conversation would stop there; Mme Giraud would have nothing more to say. Only one person, because of her extreme shrewdness, her life experience, her unique personality, and the genuine influence she had over Paule, could talk to her and lead her to understand that not all the wrongdoing was mine and that, in fact, mine was to some extent the direct result of hers. But I hesitated to bring Mme de Blangy into our marital quarrels, to make her the confidante of my domestic troubles. I was afraid of her type of intelligence, her mocking humor, the barbs she would not fail to aim at me, and even her point-blank way of looking at me.

XI

I was wrong. Mme de Blangy, whom I decided one day to make my confidante, proved herself to be completely good-natured. She was happy to let me tell her all my troubles; she didn't let me leave out the slightest detail. Far from finding my stories tiresome, she seemed to enjoy listening to them, to take some sort of pleasure in them, and when I had finished, she cried, "I was a little prejudiced against you at first, but now I sympathize with you completely."

I gave these words the simplest of explanations. "As my wife's best friend," I told myself, "Mme de Blangy must have feared that Paule would give me all the affection she had been giving her. My secrets have reassured her; she knows now that Paule does not love me, and that Paule was telling the truth when she promised to love her forever: her jealousy has disappeared and she approves of me again."

Indeed, she tried to help me search for reasons why my wife might have become alienated from me. She could not find a one.

We also looked for a way for me to get out of the ambiguous position I was in, but despite all her intelligence, Mme de Blangy couldn't think of one. She nonetheless found me so inconsolable, so beaten down, that she took pity on me and ended up saying, "I am going away for three days, to visit a relative in Le Havre. If you're willing to entrust your wife to me, I will spend all my time taking her to task, trying to set her back on the right path, teaching her how to love you."

I accepted with gratitude and hurried off to find Paule and propose that she pack her trunk as quickly as possible. The idea of the trip seemed to delight her, and she immediately went to her friend's house to set the date for their departure. It took place the very next day, and I accompanied the two ladies to the Rue d'Amsterdam station.

"I have high hopes," Mme de Blangy said to me, shaking my hand as she was climbing into the train. "I will bring her back to you completely transformed."

I was not aware of any transformation. The trip failed to change my situation in any way. I had reason to believe, however, that there was a certain change in Paule's expression, that Mme de Blangy had indeed harassed her, scolded her about me, and swamped her with lectures. But it was a fact that nothing could win out over that indomitable character.

It was then, my dear friend, that I—irritated, annoyed, unnerved, having become cruel—gave free rein to the tyranny I have already mentioned.

As long as I had had some hope, I had held back in spite of my nervous tension and my genuine sorrow. I hadn't wanted any of the blame to fall on me, and although I hadn't had all the kindnesses of a loving and beloved husband for Paule, she certainly had no cause for complaint about me either. I left her free to spend her time as she pleased, to see whom she wished; I provided her with enough distraction, and more than once I had brought her some sort of gift, hoping to touch her heart.

As of her return from the trip, however, I refused to accompany her when she wanted to go out; I pretended to have business to conduct on the days when she wanted to go to a concert or a play. I no longer escorted her to social functions and closed my door to visitors. I cut back on household expenses.

What can I say? I had no idea what else to do! Having tried in vain to win her over with kindness, I tried to starve her out.

Paule, I give her this, never complained about the way I treated her; she never uttered a reproach or a critical remark. She seemed to make a point of being as submissive, in certain situations, as she was not in others. She was no doubt aware of how wrong her behavior was toward me, and she sought to redeem it through her good humor and the charm of an always lively, always amiable, wit.

Even jealousy had no power over her unshakable serenity. Yes, jealousy! As a last resort, I tried to make Paule jealous.

That was madness, you will say, and I completely agree with you. A married man, I took a mistress, an official mistress, I who as a bachelor had had only the most passing and mysterious liaisons (if they can even be called liaisons). I allowed a famous courtesan, known by everyone in Paris, to show me off as her lover; I even asked her to do it, as a favor. I left letters that she had written me lying around the house and sent her my responses by way of a servant. One day, at the dinner table, in front of Paule, I paid a bill of six hundred francs for diamond earrings that I had given, that morning, to Mlle X. In short, dear friend, I cheated on my wife; yes, I cheated on her.

You will respond that my wife could not have been much aware of the situation. I beg your pardon: I came home so late at night, making so much noise, that the entire household knew of my immorality. I had become cynical!

You might think that when I started creating a scandal, Paule would have felt obliged to express her unhappiness to me, at least for the sake of form. You would be wrong: she was never so amiable, so eager to please me.

The more she overwhelmed me with her indifference and her indulgence, the more enraged I became, the harder I tried to cause her pain, to move her, in order to pull her out of her apathy. Finally, I thought I had found a way to be disagreeable to her and to force her perhaps to ask for my mercy. It was to separate her from her best friend, Mme de Blangy, at whose home, since I had begun to neglect her, she spent her afternoons and almost all her evenings.

One day, when she was getting ready to go out, I stopped her, saying, "Where are you going?"

"As usual, to my mother's for a minute, then to Berthe's."

"I think you go to Mme de Blangy's far too often."

She suddenly raised her head, looked at me, and said, "Why do you say that?"

"Because . . ."

Fishing for something to say and not really finding anything, I said, "Because the countess's company is not appropriate; she's far too worldly a woman for you."

"Berthe? Worldly? She scarcely receives a few visits and makes the fewest possible herself, and she never goes out to parties."

"Obviously. She wouldn't be comfortable there. Her status as a separated woman, as a married woman who . . . *isn't*, puts her in a difficult situation."

"But everyone knows that it's all her husband's fault."

"Not at all. Many people doubt that; I, for example. Has experience not shown that, in certain marriages, the first wrongdoing comes from the wife? I have given this a lot of thought: being in Mme de Blangy's company could compromise a woman as young as you, a young girl, so to speak."

"It certainly took you long enough to figure this out," she said, without seeming to pay attention to my allusions.

"I would probably never have noticed if I hadn't been so cruelly disappointed by you."

She didn't even deign to acknowledge this last comment, and began again. "I thought the countess was your friend."

"She's too much your friend to be mine as well."

"Which doesn't stop you from going to ask her for favors."

"Which she doesn't perform."

"It's not up to her."

"Too bad. A woman of her age, experience, and position should have much more influence over you."

"Oh, she has quite a bit."

"Then she uses it badly, which means that she's all the more dangerous."

Clearly I had succeeded in getting a reaction from Paule; for the first time, she was arguing with me. Thus I became increasingly bold with each of her responses. Perhaps I had found her weak spot: her friendship with Mme de Blangy, her fear of losing her, might well make her decide to give in to me.

After a moment, she began again. "What conclusion should I draw from everything you've just said?"

"Oh!" I said, having decided to strike a sudden, stunning blow, "the simplest conclusion of all: you will no longer see the countess."

"Really? Not at all?"

"Not at all."

"And what if I wanted to continue seeing her?" she cried, abandoning altogether, this time, her usual calm.

"I would prevent you from doing so," I responded.

"How?"

"First, I would give orders to my servants never to receive Mme de Blangy, and they would obey me."

"I don't doubt it. But even if I don't see her here, I can always see her at her house."

"That would be equally impossible."

"Do you intend to lock me up?"

"I hadn't planned on it."

"What then?"

"I will simply go see the countess and say to her, 'I ask you, madame, to please cease having any contact with my wife.'"

"And if she refuses?"

"She can't refuse. Her status as a separated woman obliges her to be very careful, extremely circumspect. She knows that she would quickly begin to lose her social standing if it became known that in spite of the expressed will of a husband, she continued to invite his wife to her house. In polite society, there are certain customs and certain rules that one cannot disregard without ceasing to be accepted by that society."

Paule must have understood how right I was; she remained silent.

She didn't break her silence until a moment had passed, and then said, "May I at least make one last visit to Mme de Blangy, to inform her of your wishes and express my regret at not being able to see her anymore?"

"Certainly," I said, touched in spite of myself by this submission to my desires.

When she had left, I told myself that the submission was only a facade. Paule, without a doubt, was going to conspire with the countess to find a way of making me change my mind. What did I care? Was I not determined not to weaken, to be merciless as long as I was being given no mercy?

I was wrong on that point as well. Paule never opened her mouth again about Mme de Blangy; Mme de Blangy, for her part, made no attempt whatsoever to persuade me to return her friend to her. She did not even write to me, as I had expected, to reproach me for my behavior toward her. I didn't have to banish her from my door, as she never came to knock, and I had solid proof that Paule was no longer going to her house. Indeed, didn't Mme de Blangy live on our street, nearly directly across from us, and when my wife went out, couldn't I watch her with my own eyes from the window, hidden behind the shutters, and thus convince myself that she passed the countess's house without going in?

"This situation cannot last!" I told myself. "They are too proud to come to me and beg me to give them their former life back. They are both counting on time, on reflection, on my love, to make me take pity on them; but when they realize that they can't count on those things, then . . ."

How wretched I was! To hold on with such ferocity to a woman who didn't want me!

My nerves had perhaps never been more strained than during that period. My desire had never been more acute.

My liaison with Mlle X had no doubt brought about this result; beside the woman you do not love, you are always tempted to think about the one you do. You see her, you hear her, you say to yourself, "What if it were her?" Your mind is enflamed, and the one who was supposed to cure you of your love for another ends up only making that love stronger.

XII

Time passed, and Paule regained all her placidity. She even seemed to forget Mme de Blangy; above all, she forgot that I was her husband. Nonetheless, I hoped, I continued to hope.

I was counting on my tyranny, on the kind of seclusion in which my wife was living, and on the desire she must have had to see her best friend again.

Soon I hoped no more; here's what happened:

I had just had lunch alone with Paule. While I was reading the newspapers in the drawing room, she went into her dressing room. She came out a few minutes later, with a cloak around her shoulders and a hat on her head, and said to me, "I am going to run some errands; I'm also going up to see my mother. Is there anything I can do for you while I'm out?"

"No, thank you," I answered.

"Good-bye, then," she added and then left.

When the door to the apartment closed, I ran to my usual post, to the lookout I had created for myself behind one of the shutters in the study, the room that had (alas!) become my bachelor's quarters.

It was purely out of habit that I went to the trouble of doing this. For two months at that point, Paule had passed by Mme de Blangy's house without stopping, without even raising her eyes toward her friend's windows; she had no reason, that particular day, to do any differently. I soon saw her on the sidewalk below me; she walked past the houses, in the direction of the boulevard. I caught myself admiring her: her hair, held up in the back by a fine net, had dazzling highlights in the sunshine. From time to time, to avoid some obstacle, she lifted the hem of her dress with an almost imperceptible gesture, and you could see two deliciously arched feet and a little bit of an adorable leg.

She wasn't walking so much as undulating, so to speak: her shoulders, her waist, her hips seemed to roll from right to left and from left to right. It was extraordinarily seductive.

All of a sudden, an insane thought occurred to me: "If I follow her," I told myself, "I will be able to watch her longer."

I swear to you, dear friend, that it was not jealousy speaking to me at that moment (at least I don't think so): I was charmed, I wanted to stay under the spell, that's all. I had forgotten that Paule was my wife; indeed, nothing was easier to forget.

I ran quickly down the stairs. I was sure I could find her. Rue Caumartin is long and straight and there are very few cross streets.

I hadn't gone more than twenty steps toward the boulevards when I saw in front of me, on the same sidewalk, my little feet, my bit of leg, my hair, my nape of neck, my shoulders, and my back. All of it continued to undulate: I followed the undulations.

When Paule got to the end of Rue Caumartin, before crossing Rue Basse-du-Rempart, she seemed to be trying to make up her mind. Was she going to head toward the Madeleine or toward the Bastille? Suddenly, before deciding, and as if obeying a recommendation from someone, she turned and looked behind her.

I barely had time to duck into a carriage entrance; she didn't see me.

No doubt reassured, she took the boulevard and began walking toward the Madeleine.

But her uncertain way of walking, her gestures, the look behind her, the kind of worry she seemed to be experiencing at that moment all gave me pause.

"Is she afraid of being followed?" I wondered.

I was starting to get jealous, which was all I needed at that point! Perhaps you are surprised, dear friend, that I was not already jealous. You are wrong; I couldn't be jealous. Since our wedding, Paule's had been the most ordered and the least varied of lives: she made few visits, rarely received any, and only left the house, as I have said, to go see her mother or her friend.

Give or take a half hour here or there, I had always known where she was at all times. How, under those circumstances, could one suspect a woman of infidelity, how could one be jealous? When I tried to find a reason for her behavior toward me, it had of course occurred to me to think, "Could she have a lover?" But I immediately had to admit that she could not, unless her rendezvous took place in our apartment, her mother's place, or Mme de Blangy's. All three possibilities were out of the question.

When she got to the Place de la Madeleine, Paule headed toward the church; she went through the gate and up the steps. "What does this mean?" I said to myself.

"So she's going to church in the middle of the week now, the same woman who doesn't even consider going to mass on Sunday?"

I added, "Do I have piety to thank for my torment? Could someone have inflicted a penance on my wife, a penance that she's imposing on me as well? Could we both be victims of one of those vows spoken in a distraught moment? In that case, there is hope! No one takes eternal vows anymore, it might be only temporary."

I sprang off toward the Madeleine market. A new thought had just occurred to me: Paule had gone into the church just to lose anyone who might have been trying to follow her, and she would leave by one of the side doors.

Why did I rush to the right rather than to the left? I have no idea, but my choice was a felicitous one. I had barely had the time to hide behind one of the little stalls used by the flower sellers, when I saw my wife. She had only passed through the church, as one would cross a public square. And to think that I had suspected her, just a minute earlier, of piety!

There was no longer any room for illusion: she was on her way to a rendezvous. She was simply going there by a roundabout route.

She took off on her path again, and I followed. I kept a good thirty paces behind her, always watchful, ready to fade away like a shadow if ever she turned around. Jealousy had just transformed me into the most expert of policemen.

Now she was walking along Boulevard des Capucines and walking rather quickly. From time to time, I was overwhelmed by an insane feeling of terror: what if all the passersby, going in all different directions, hid her from my sight? What if I lost her? So I got closer, I ran, I suddenly found myself two steps away from her, behind some great big character perfectly suited to serve as a living wall.

At Boulevard des Italiens, I almost lost her. I thought I saw her head toward Rue de la Chaussée d'Antin. A quick glance right and left convinced me I was wrong; I went back to the boulevard and caught up with her just as she was turning onto Rue Helder.

My position was increasingly dangerous: the street Paule had taken is not heavily traveled, the sidewalks are narrow, the carriage entrances sometimes closed, and the stores few and far between. It would be difficult to hide suddenly; the least bit of negligence on my part could betray me. There was none, thanks to the skills that had suddenly arisen in me, skills that would certainly have been much appreciated at police headquarters. Instead of following my wife from a few feet away as I had been doing, I followed her with my eyes and didn't begin walking again until she reached Rue Taitbout. At that point, I could safely take cover in the shadows again.

Where *were* we going, when were we going to stop? For a minute or so, certain clues led me to believe that I was nearing the end of my wanderings. Paule seemed more worried, her steps were less regular, she was turning around more often. She did not feel she was being followed, but she was no doubt telling herself that the time had come to increase her caution. Oh, dear friend, such a trek, such a chase, such a hunt, and, especially, such emotions!

Finally, after having turned right onto Rue de Provence, passed Rue Saint-Georges, and crossed Boulevard Lafayette, she turned onto Rue Laffitte, and I saw her suddenly disappear into a carriage entrance.

I stopped. What was I going to do? Go into the house she had just entered, catch up to her on the stairs, reproach her for her behavior, treat her as she deserved to be treated, and force her to come with me?

But then her secret would elude me: she would refuse to admit that she was going to a rendezvous. She would use the first possible pretext to explain her presence in this unknown house: she had been given the address of some supplier and was looking for him. She had gone into the Madeleine to pray; she turned around every minute in the street out of curiosity; she walked all over Paris before going to Rue Laffitte just because she loved to stroll. Oh, she would have had no trouble coming up with answers, I can promise you that. She would have managed to confuse me; perhaps she would even have convinced me of her innocence.

Was it a good idea to go see the concierge? He must know her; this was surely not the first time she had been in the house. But what if the man was loyal to her, if he refused to answer me, if he warned her?

In that case, I would learn nothing; I would have no proof of her treachery; I would not know the name of the man who had dishonored me; and I could take my revenge on neither him nor her!

Ah, revenge! What a pleasure, after having suffered so much!

In the best interest of my revenge, I decided to be calm, patient, clever. I decided to wait.

To wait! To wait at that door, in front of that house, where, I was sure, she was cheating on me, betraying me, giving to another man everything that she had refused to give to me! What torture!

An empty carriage passed by at that moment and I signaled the coachman to pull over at the corner of Rue Laffitte and Rue de la Victoire. I got into the carriage, opened the windows, and, my eyes fixed on the carriage entrance through which Paule had gone, waited.

Two hours went by. Two hours!

At last, she came out. There was a heavy veil over her face, one of those woolen ones called English veils, used by adulterous women. She stopped at the doorstep, appeared to be looking around, hesitated to brave the street, and then, making up her mind, went off quickly in the direction of the boulevards.

As for me, I stayed for a while at my observation post: perhaps I was going to see the man she had just left.

No one appeared, or rather my suspicions couldn't latch onto any of the people I saw come out.

I got out of the carriage, sent the coachman away, and went back home.

Paule was already ensconced in the drawing room.

"You're certainly getting home late!" she said.

I was about to explode, but I held myself back.

"Have you been waiting for me long?" I asked.

"Long enough."

"Were you satisfied with your outing?"

"Very satisfied; the weather was so nice! I took advantage of it to run several errands."

"Did you see your mother?"

"No, she had gone out. I will see her this evening, if you permit me to."

"Certainly."

It was announced that dinner was served; I offered Paule my arm, and we went into the dining room.

XIII

Do not be surprised, dear friend, by how cool I was or how well I managed to control myself that sad day. I was less to be pitied than you think.

Yes, less to be pitied: at last, I was no longer walking in darkness, I was no longer surrounded by mystery, I no longer had to look for the reasons behind her indifference and her coldness. I now had the answer to the riddle that I had been determined to guess for so long; I was no longer gazing at a sphinx, I was in the presence of a woman constituted like all of them, unfaithful like most of them. In a word, I could no longer doubt: Paule had refused my love because she had a lover.

Oh, it was awful of course and I did suffer cruelly, but at least I knew the nature of my pain, the name of my illness. I was surely going to know the identity of the man who had reduced me to despair, who had dared take my property from me, who had seized my rights, who had stolen a heart that belonged to me, to keep it for himself alone, without consenting to the tiniest bit of sharing.

The wretch! He had probably told her, "I will consent to your marrying him, to his giving you his name, but I alone will in truth be your husband. You will not take his love and his rights into account at all. You will love only me."

Yes, he had told her that, and had dragged some solemn vow out of her. Otherwise, she would have behaved like most married women with a lover: she would have cheated on me with him and cheated on him with me.

But who was he? I had to see him, know him, as soon as possible. I had to . . .

Oh, dear friend, my imagination had never caused me much pain, but if you only knew how feverishly it was working now, how it was spinning out of control, the revenge scenarios to which it was driving me! I assure you that my former classmates would not have made fun of my peace-loving nature, as they used to, at that moment. My ferocity would have terrified them.

Alas, I had no chance to put that ferocity into practice, either the next day or the day after. Paule did not go out. It was probably not the appointed day for a rendezvous. Their passions were intermittent. I was distressed.

To be reduced to despair by my wife's *relative* virtue!

Finally, the third day, after lunch, she announced plans for a walk.

"Which way are you heading?" I asked.

"I'm not sure," she said. "Wherever my mood takes me; probably where there are some stores."

"Do you want me to come with you?"

She replied without batting an eye, "Nothing would please me more; I'll put on my hat and be right back."

What skill in throwing off my suspicions, what clever deceitfulness! Had I been less aware of the situation, I could easily have believed that I wasn't disturbing her plans in any way.

I was the one who had to pull back, on the pretext of some business matter, in order to let her go out alone.

This time I wasn't imprudent enough to follow her. Didn't I already know where she was going?

I hired a carriage and had myself driven to the spot where I had posted myself on lookout before.

According to my calculations, I had some time ahead of me; it would take her more than an hour to make her usual detours and circuits before getting to Rue Laffitte.

Several messengers were hanging around looking for work at the corner of Rue Laffitte and Rue de la Victoire. From my carriage, I called out to the one whose intelligent face made him seem like the best bet.

"How would you like to earn a little pocket money?" I said to the man.

An affirmative answer came forth without any hesitation.

I continued like this: "You will stand next to my carriage, as if you were chatting with the coachman. When I touch your arm, you will immediately look in front of you, and you will see a woman going into that building over there, the third one on the right. You will wait several seconds, then you will catch up with the woman on the stairs, come back here, and tell me which floor she stopped on. As you can see, nothing could be simpler; the only thing is, the person in question mustn't have any idea that she's being followed. You will take care not to stop on the same floor she does, and to have a piece of paper in your hand to make it look as if you've been hired to deliver a message in the building."

I didn't have to repeat myself; my man had understood everything.

About fifteen minutes later, I saw Paule. I gave the agreed-upon signal, the messenger interrupted the conversation he had started up with the coachman, and, after a brief pause, entered the house my wife had gone into.

Five minutes later, he came back to me.

"Well?" I asked.

"The woman," he answered, "stopped on the third floor."

"Which side?"

"The side with the little apartments that look out over the courtyard, on the right as you're going up."

"She must have rung a doorbell. Who opened the door for her?"

"She didn't ring. As she was going up the stairs, she took a little key out of her change purse and then opened the door herself."

This last detail changed my suspicions into certainties.

"Very good," I said as I gave the messenger the agreed-upon louis. In order to be sure of the man's discretion, I added, "I may need you again for the same price."

That day, my wife cut her visit short and, consequently, my guard duty.

When I had watched her go out of sight, I left the carriage and headed for the building she had just come out of.

In order to make contact with the concierge, I would have to rely on the most vulgar kind of ruse, but those are the ones that most often work.

"Do you have an apartment for rent?" I said to a woman in the concierge's office.

"Yes, sir, on the fifth floor. We have another on the third floor."

"Ah, the one on the third floor would suit me better. In the front or the back of the building?"

"In the front; it's a five-thousand-franc apartment."

"A small apartment then?" I said self-assuredly.

The concierge, who had remained seated while answering my questions, got up. The kind of person who, far from being scared off by a price of five thousand francs, actually found it too low, deserved to be shown some respect.

"The apartment is certainly not huge, sir," she said. "There are more impressive ones, especially in the new neighborhoods. But it does have four bedrooms."

"Alas!" I responded, having decided on a plan even as I spoke. "I need five."

"There is a small drawing room that the gentleman could make into a bedroom. Would the gentleman care to see it?"

"All right then, let's take a look."

Just as I had figured, according to my messenger's report, two doors opened onto the third-floor landing. A big double door, which led into the apartment that I was going to visit; on the right, a smaller one with a copper lock.

I followed the concierge and conscientiously walked through all the rooms that she opened for me.

When my inspection was over, I said, "It's a shame; in many ways, this apartment is just what I am looking for.

It's perfectly situated; it's airy. Were it not for my son, I would not hesitate to rent it."

I dared give myself a son, I who didn't even have a wife.

"The gentleman's son wouldn't like it here?" asked the concierge, intrigued by my words.

"He would complain about being under the same roof with me, about not having his own entrance. My son is a bachelor; he consents to living at home, but on the condition that he be able to enjoy a bit of freedom. If there were, for example, on the same floor as this one, a little two- or three-room apartment, that would be perfect. Unfortunately, there are no small apartments in this building."

"I beg your pardon, sir," replied the concierge. "On the contrary, each floor has apartments that rent for anywhere from eight hundred to twelve hundred francs. But there are none for rent right now."

"What a shame! The apartment across from this one would have suited me so well! I have been looking for an arrangement like this for a long time."

I played my role with such conviction that the concierge, as I had hoped, said, "We could probably work something out. The owner wants to rent the big apartment and, if it suits the gentleman and the gentleman absolutely insists on having the small one as well, we could simply give notice to the tenant across the hall."

"Oh, to disturb someone who has lived in the building for a long time for the sake of a newcomer . . ."

"No, sir; this is a person who has been here for only two months."

"Ah, two months! All the same, this person must have got comfortable, developed a routine."

"Not really. This person lives in the country, it seems, and has taken the apartment as a pied-à-terre. This is a person who takes a few minutes of rest here while in Paris, two or three times a week."

"It is no doubt a young man who lives at home," I said, smiling, "and has his amorous rendezvous here."

"No, sir," said the concierge, "it's a woman."

A woman! I was astounded. My wife had been bold enough to rent this apartment, in which to receive her lover, herself. I could no longer even tell myself that, driven by passion, she had consented to go to the apartment of the man who had succeeded in making her love him, that she had succumbed little by little, as many women succumb. No! She had arranged her own downfall, she was its creator; like Marguerite of Burgundy, she possessed her own little Tour de Nesle.

The concierge began again. "If the gentleman wishes, I will go see the tenant as soon as tomorrow and I am sure that the matter can be arranged."

"I couldn't ask for anything more," I said, getting a grip on myself, "but I wonder if I could have a glimpse of the apartment you've been telling me about. It would be difficult for me to rent it without knowing how it was laid out."

"Nothing could be simpler; I do the cleaning for the woman, so she gave me a key. If the gentleman would like to go in . . ."

"How about today? I have the time."

"Today is impossible. Madame is in Paris. I saw her go up the stairs."

"And she hasn't left yet?"

"I don't think so, sir."

This concierge was clearly very bad at her job. The third-floor tenant had gone out an hour ago without anyone's having noticed. My wife had been lucky in choosing this building.

But it was not my place to press the point.

"What about tomorrow?" I said. "Could I visit the apartment in question then?"

"Certainly, sir. Madame never comes to Paris two days in a row."

"See you tomorrow then, and since I hope to be your tenant soon, please accept this little sum as a tip for you from a newcomer to the building."

I was eager to make the woman my ally.

XIV

I was prompt for the appointment: the next day, around two o'clock, I was once again on Rue Laffitte. As soon as she saw me, the concierge, remembering the gratuity I had given her, greeted me with her most gracious smile, came out of her office, and preceded me up the stairs. When we reached the third floor, she took a pretty little steel key out of her pocket, put it into a Fichet lock, and stepped aside so that I could go in.

How my heart was beating, how I suffered entering those mysterious quarters! I was about to see the place that had witnessed pleasures only I should have known. I would actually be touching, so to speak, my wife's betrayal and vile deeds.

After walking through two rooms, I stopped and asked the concierge, "Isn't this apartment furnished?"

"I told the gentleman that it is a pied-à-terre; madame never sleeps here. When she comes during the day, she spends her time in the drawing room."

"Where is the drawing room?"

"Here it is."

I pushed open a door and went in.

At first I couldn't see anything. The shutters were closed and the curtains were drawn. The concierge ran to the window and threw everything open. I gaped.

Picture, dear friend, a small room about four meters square, a boudoir more than a drawing room, with walls upholstered in black satin, tufted with buttons of flame red. One of those huge Turkish-style sofas—very low, almost on the ground in fact, covered with a fabric similar to the one on the walls and tufted the same way—went all around the perimeter of the room. On the parquet floor was a thick carpet with a triple pad under it, as well as black satin cushions from the sofa, scattered here and there to serve as seats. The only decoration on the walls were several little Venetian mirrors and charming Louis XV wall sconces that held half-burned pink candles. In the middle of the mantel, a small marble reproduction of Falconnet's bathing woman; to its left and right, two groups of Clodion figurines, in terra-cotta. Across from the mantel, a set of shelves in ebony, with mother-of-pearl inlay, holding a rock-crystal goblet full of Turkish cigarettes and several books bound in red leather, the titles of which I skimmed quickly. They were, if I remember correctly, a volume of Balzac containing *A Passion in the Desert* and *The Girl with the Golden Eyes*; *Mlle de Maupin*, by Théophile Gautier; Diderot's *The Nun*; and the latest novel by Ernest Feydeau, *Mme de Chalis*.

There you have, dear friend, the exact description of the lodging. The unusual nature of the furnishings and the strangeness of certain details didn't strike me until much later, when I was called upon to think back on the place.

After visiting the boudoir, I asked the concierge if there weren't any other rooms.

"There's a dressing room," she told me.

Steeling myself, I went in, expecting some eccentric setup.

I was wrong: the room was barely furnished. There were chintz curtains at the windows; on a little marble table were a Bohemian glass washbasin, a blond tortoiseshell comb, and a box of rice powder.

"This room isn't very big," the concierge said, "but it's very useful, because of the closets."

"Closets! Let's take a look."

Surely I would penetrate the mystery and find myself looking at clothes that would provide me with some information about my rival.

However, on the pretext of trying to figure out exactly how deep the closet was, I looked in every corner without finding the least little frock coat, overcoat, or even suit coat. I did see, hanging on a coatrack, a large shawl-type garment, like those worn by women in ancient Greece, made of white cashmere and lined with satin of the same flame-red hue I had already noticed in the boudoir, as well as a large dressing gown of black satin, lined and quilted inside with pearl-gray satin.

Shall I go ahead and admit my latest weakness to you? The fact is, I could not take my eyes off these clothes, which obviously belonged to my wife and which were still completely impregnated with heady perfumes. I imagined the shawl opening, revealing her glorious torso, her breasts so firm, her arched back, her accentuated hips, as they had appeared to me, one single night, in all their magnificent nudity. The flame-red of the shawl, or the pearl-gray of the dressing gown, emphasized the whiteness of her skin and cast deep shadows on that adorable body.

My wandering imagination went even further: suddenly I saw Paule step out of her shawl, as Ingres's odalisque might step out of her frame, and, quivering with emotion, walk toward the man she preferred to me.

Oh, what I would have given to be in that man's place! What I am about to confess to you is unworthy, it is cowardly: I think if someone had said to me, at that moment, "You have found out everything, the guilty parties have been shamed, forgive them, don't exercise your legal rights, and your wife will be your wife. She will wear this shawl, that she once wore for another, for you. She will come join you in the boudoir sparkling with light and silk. For a week, a day, an hour, her smiles, her kisses, her caresses will be yours; all the sensual pleasures that you have dreamed of since your marriage, but have eluded you, will be yours," I would have forgiven her!

I know that not everyone will understand me. People will be tempted to say, "You cannot still love that woman. When you found out what you just found out, when you discovered her betrayal, scorn must have killed your love." Well, in certain cases, desire lives on after love, and only possession can kill desire!

The emotions I experienced during my visit to Rue Laffitte left me several hours later. I went home completely in control of myself, no longer feeling anything other than the outrage that befits a husband, a man cruelly wounded in his pride.

Two long days went by, during which Paule didn't seem interested in going out. Her memories must have been enough for her and must have helped her wait patiently for the next rendezvous.

At last the time came. I watched her leave, lighthearted and calm, a thousand miles away from guessing what was taking place inside me.

She had scarcely left before I went downstairs myself.

Ten minutes later, I was on Rue Laffitte. I intended to follow, point by point, the plan I had set out for myself.

"I asked you for forty-eight hours to think it over," I told the concierge. "I've almost made up my mind. There are just a few details about my moving in that keep me from officially committing to the larger apartment. I would like to install some old sideboards and some antique tapestries that I wouldn't want to have to trim or cut under any circumstances, so it's important that I find out whether they will fit in the drawing room. I have taken their exact measurements, and if you don't object, now I'd like to measure the height of the walls."

In order to lend more credibility to what I was saying, I pulled from my pocket a paper with numbers written all over it.

The concierge found my request perfectly natural and hurried off to open the apartment that I was about to rent. Since it was totally empty, she thought nothing of leaving me alone with my calculations and returning to her office.

At last! I was free! Through the door to the landing, I was going to see, any minute, Paule come up the stairs and step onto the landing. Perhaps her lover was already waiting for her and would come to the door to greet her; at that point, I would rush at him. Perhaps she was going to meet him later; the moment he put his key in the lock, I would find myself face to face with him, block him from going in, and ask him for satisfaction.

After about fifteen minutes, I heard footsteps on the stairs.

I opened the door a crack: no one could see me, but I could see perfectly.

It was my wife. She was walking up the stairs briskly, like a person eager to get somewhere or afraid of being followed; crossing the landing, she came so close to me that I heard the sound of her rapid breathing. Standing perfectly still, with one hand holding back the door and the other holding my heart, which was about to explode, I watched her.

She pulled a key from her pocket and opened the door.

No one came to meet her; no voice welcomed her.

She was the first to arrive for the rendezvous; the other person would come later, or else he was already there and hadn't heard her open the door.

This last theory must have been the right one: forty-five minutes went by and several people came up the stairs, but none stopped on the landing. It was unlikely that anyone would make my wife wait so long.

Then the shawl lined with flame-red satin appeared in my mind. Despite the three doors that separated me from

Paule, I saw her take off her ordinary clothes and slip into the sensual garment. In the process, she had gotten cold and her flesh shivered at the touch of the satin; she rushed into the boudoir upholstered in silk and curled up in front of the fire, on downy cushions; the shawl fell partly open and the flame from the hearth warmed her beautiful body, caressed it with reflections of reddish light. My rival, full of wonder, crazed, ran to her and took her in his arms.

Yes, I saw all that, and I was overcome with mindless rage. I rushed to break down the obstacles between them and me; I wanted to appear to them all of a sudden, to surprise them in the middle of their ecstasy, to strike them, to kill them!

But good sense told me, "Calm down, take care: by the time you get to them, by the time you break down all those doors, they will have had time to be on their guard. The noise will bring the neighbors running, they'll think you're a criminal or a madman, you might be arrested and *he* will escape! Just suffer through it a little while longer, he's going to have to come out eventually, and then . . . you will have your revenge!"

I waited. Another forty-five minutes went by.

At last, a door opened, then another; I heard the sound of a voice.

He was coming out with her! I was going to see him.

The door to the landing opened; my wife appeared. While she was slowly pushing the door open, in order to make her way out, someone was holding it back from the inside. At the same time, I heard these words, "I promise, day after tomorrow at the latest, and I'll try to stay longer."

At that moment, I sprang out: with one hand I forcefully held my wife aside, with the other I pushed open the door that they hadn't had time to close, and I found myself face to face with . . .

XV

Imagine my astonishment: I found myself face to face with Mme de Blangy.

Speechless, I looked at her without saying a word.

She herself seemed quite upset. My tempestuous entrance had been reason enough to upset her.

She nonetheless got hold of herself before I did, opened the door all the way, and, speaking to Paule, who had stayed on the landing, said, "It's your husband, my dear; he appeared so suddenly that perhaps you didn't recognize him. You no longer have any need to rush off."

When Paule had closed the door behind her, Mme de Blangy, turning to me, said, this time in her most natural voice, "I am delighted, sir, to receive you in my humble lodgings. Please follow me."

Since I didn't answer, she took Paule's arm and walked ahead of me.

I followed them.

We went into the boudoir.

At that point I was able to speak. I might just as well have kept silent, since the only thing I found to say was, to say the least, useless: "So this is yours!"

"What do you mean, this is mine!" she cried, laughing. "Did you doubt it? Whose apartment did you think you were entering so cavalierly? Your own? I must say, your manners would make more sense in that case. No, this is mine, definitely mine. You must be wondering why I have two residences. Actually, it's quite simple. On Rue Caumartin, I am constantly being bothered; there's always someone at my doorbell and I don't have a moment's peace. Here, I can enjoy total peace and quiet. I retreat to this humble abode, as the wise men of old retreated to the desert, to think. In this boudoir, I have all the advantages of being in the country—silence, isolation, calm, rest—without any of the disadvantages, like cocks crowing, dogs barking, or the smell of the stables. I arrange my life as it pleases me alone, dear sir: I depend on no one; I am a bachelor."

She had spouted all that off in one shot, without stopping to catch her breath, no doubt trying to confuse me with all this verbiage and dominate the situation.

She stopped to take a breath. Then, with genuine skill, she anticipated all the objections I might have made, all the astonishment I might have been feeling.

"I see you looking around, a bit flabbergasted, if you will," she said, smiling. "You are telling yourself that this boudoir is rather luxurious for a retreat, that the furnishings are rather odd. This big circular sofa, these Venetian mirrors, these figurines on the mantel, you must admit, take your breath away a little. Dear sir, the reason I put statuettes on my mantel instead of the usual clock is that first, I hate anything usual, and second, I enjoy losing track of time here. This sofa is a delightful piece of furniture, the original of which I saw in the Turkish pavilion at the Universal Exposition. Come on, stretch out a little, you'll see how comfortable it is. As for the mirrors, you would have admired them lavishly, if you had made your little . . . invasion into my home a half hour ago. At that point, the candles were lit, the fire was dancing, a thousand glimmers of light were reflected in all these little mirrors; it was divine. But I was planning to leave just after Paule, I was far from expecting you, so I thought I could put out the fire, blow out the candles, and let the sun come in. Poor thing, it has no effect here . . . please forgive it."

I didn't need Mme de Blangy's admonition about forgiving the sun; it wasn't the sun I was angry at.

As a matter of fact, at whom was I angry? I didn't know anymore. The countess had succeeded in confusing me. My head was spinning. As she talked about the mantel and the sofa and the mirrors, my eyes went from each spot and object to the next. Now I was looking blankly at the famous shawl that I took such pains to describe to you: I spied it spread out casually on the sofa, near where Paule was sitting. It belonged of course to Mme de Blangy. And to think what a vivid impression it had made on me! Intoxicated, I had caressed the satin; I had deliciously breathed in the smells that emanated from it; I had dreamed of it. Such is imagination!

One might really have believed that the countess could read my mind.

"You're admiring my shawl," she said, suddenly. "As well you should. It's a delightful garment to wear around the house."

She got up, took the shawl, and put it on over her clothes.

"See how well it fits me," she continued. "In spite of how large it is, it shows off one's chest and shoulders remarkably well. And look how gracefully the pleats fall! Paule is crazy about it, you should order one like it for her. I would have given her this one; unfortunately, we're not the same size."

Since I was nodding approvingly, without saying anything, she cried, "Have you gone mute? Here I am, trying my best to fish for compliments, and you won't deign to unclench your teeth. What *is* the matter?"

"Oh, I know!" she began again, after having thought for a moment. "To think that I didn't come up with it before! The gentleman is furious that we disobeyed him, that we transgressed his orders; he has forbidden his wife to see me again, and here she is seeing me again. He followed her and now, unfortunately, has proof of her disobedience."

She came over to sit, or rather lie, down next to me on the sofa and continued, "Come now, let's think it through a little. First, as far as I'm concerned, I can officially tell

118

you that I didn't hold a grudge against you for a single instant. You are jealous of any affection that your wife might have for anyone; you demand that she love only you. That is, at the least, presumptuous, but in and of itself it doesn't offend me. When Paule came to me, two months ago, to announce the law you had laid down concerning me, the ostracism you were imposing on me, I said, 'Poor boy! How he loves you!'

"So you see, I am a benevolent princess, or countess I should say. It is true that I would have been angrier at you if I had really thought you were going to be able to separate me from my childhood friend, if I hadn't found a way of obeying you while disobeying you, if I hadn't skillfully maneuvered around the problem.

"'He refuses to receive me?' I said to Paule. 'Alas, yes,' she sighed. 'Well, that's his right, and I banish *myself* from his door. He also forbids you to visit me?' 'Yes,' murmured the poor little thing, sighing again. 'We must obey him, my dear; you see, a husband's orders are sacred. You will no longer set foot in my home on Rue Caumartin. But he hasn't forbidden you to go to Rue Laffitte, since he doesn't know about my little country house, my retreat. You will come there, two or three times a week, and spend an hour or so with me. We'll close the shutters, light candles, stretch out on the big sofa, smoke cigarettes, and say every bad thing we can think of about your husband, to get back at him for his cruelty. It will be delightful.'

"That is what we have dared to do, dear sir. If we are guilty, take one of these cushions and smother us, as they do in Turkey. It will provide some local color. But if you forgive us for loving each other since our days in the convent and for not being able to live apart from each other, drop that forbidding expression that reminds me of Bluebeard, and take this cigarette."

She continued talking like that for more than a half hour. When we took our leave of her, neither Paule nor I had been able to get a single word in, which did not stop her from telling us, "You may come back to see me in my retreat, since the sound of your voices certainly won't disturb anything. Not that I am reproaching you for it, but you two are awfully silent and discreet."

Indeed, the only thing missing at that point would have been for her to reproach us for it.

XVI

Well then, dear friend, what do you think? Shouldn't I have been delighted? The suspicions that had been causing me so much pain for a week had taken wing and flown away, as if by magic. I had no more reason to be jealous. It was obvious that Mme de Blangy was telling the truth: she had rented that apartment to live the life of a "bachelor," as she had assured me. No eccentricity on her part would have surprised me. She had furnished the place in her own style, and now that I was thinking back on a thousand details, I was amazed that I hadn't thought of her on my first visit, with the concierge. Didn't she have a piece of furniture in her drawing room on Rue Caumartin similar to the one in black satin, stitched in flame-red? Hadn't I heard her complain, many times, about the fact that the style of large Turkish sofas hadn't been adopted by our Parisian upholsterers? And shouldn't the titles on the spines of those books, of which I had already taken note at her house, have given me pause? My wife was merely guilty, as the countess had said, of cleverly sidestepping my orders. I couldn't have any serious grounds for complaint against her—no new grounds, that is, since the old ones were still in effect. Yes, still! My situation hadn't changed!

And yet, if you can believe it, I was overcome by a deadly sadness, a melancholy that was deeper than ever. For a week, my jealousy had distracted me from my sadness: I had thought of nothing but revenge, duels, and death. And now, suddenly, that jealousy had no more raison d'être; I was forced to abandon all my plans for . . . combat and return to the status quo. My awful obsession took hold of me again, and I found myself alone with the enigma that tortured me night and day.

The social distractions I had tried to enjoy had done nothing for me. I had broken up long before with the creature I told you about: that kind of relationship turned my stomach, the cure was worse than the illness.

The idea of traveling occurred to me. I told myself, "Movement, noise, new horizons to look at, having to attend to a lot of details, to talk about things that are indifferent to me, to live actively, will perhaps make me forget. In any case, even if I can't control my thoughts, even if I take them with me and cruel memories chase after me, I will still be leaving behind, at least materially, the little world I live in; that counts for something."

My preparations for departure didn't take long. Whom was I leaving behind? Just one person, the one who bore my name, and she was precisely the person from whom I wanted to get away. Perhaps I was still nurturing some vague hope? I told myself that the trip would make her think things over, since my presence had always managed to put me in the wrong. Contrary to the old saying, perhaps absence would put me in the right.[1]

Having packed my trunks for me, my valet left the room, and I was putting some papers in order, when my wife came in.

"So it is true," she said, "I was not misinformed, you are leaving on a trip?"

"As you can see."

"Without letting me know?"

---

[1] A reference to the French saying "Les absents ont toujours tort" ("Those who are absent are always in the wrong").

"I was going to say good-bye. I thought it would be pointless to upset you ahead of time."

She did not seem to note the irony in my words. Standing next to the fireplace, her elbow resting on the marble, she was watching me, in silence, make the final preparations for my departure. Then I heard her murmur these words, "Yes, perhaps it's for the best."

I put down the overnight bag I was holding in my hand and, approaching her, said, "You think I'm right to go away. My presence bothers you, doesn't it?"

"You've misunderstood what I meant," she said, gently. "I was thinking something else, something that was not at all unkind toward you."

"So you were hoping," I said, "that this trip would change your feelings about me?"

She didn't answer the question; it was probably too direct. She did say, a moment later, "It's winter. Won't you mind the cold?"

"No, I'm heading to the South."

"When do you expect to come back?" she asked.

"When you will be for me what you are supposed to be."

I expected her to answer, "I am a thoughtful companion, a faithful friend. I try to make your life easy; I have a charming personality and an even temper. What can you reproach me for?" And then, before leaving, I would have given myself the sweet satisfaction of saying to her, "I didn't marry you to have you as my social companion and to admire your personality. I respect your intellectual qualities, but I wouldn't mind knowing, in a more intimate way, your other qualities as well." In fact, I would have said that much and more; I would have exploded. That's always a bit of a relief.

She did not provide me with an excuse for exploding, however: either she was afraid of what I might say and wanted to avoid a scene or she truly was aware of how much she was in the wrong.

Nonetheless, she stayed in my room, without trying to run away from me; she watched my every move. The expression on her face showed both goodwill and sadness.

Finally, I said, "It's time for me to leave."

I rang, had my trunks carried off, and asked for a carriage.

While my orders were being followed, I remained alone with her.

We looked at each other without saying a word: I leaning against the bookshelves, she still standing near the fireplace, elbow on the marble, head in her hand.

The carriage that a servant had summoned stopped in front of the door. I took a step toward Paule and said, "Farewell."

She came toward me and bent down so that I could kiss her forehead.

Anyone watching might easily have taken her for a sister saying good-bye to her brother.

But I wasn't her brother, I adored her, I still adored her! She had been in my bedroom for an hour, next to me, despite her seeming coldness, and I hadn't stopped admiring her. A thousand times I had repeated to myself, "No woman is more charming, prettier, more accomplished, more desirable." And now, my lips trembled as they brushed her forehead; I felt, for a moment, her breasts against my chest; waves of warmth, emanating from her entire being, rose up to me.

I couldn't take it anymore. I grabbed her around the waist with one arm, trying to bend her, while I placed the other hand on her head and moved my mouth down from her forehead to her lips.

If only she had responded to this last embrace, to this desperate plea; if only her lips had opened to let out a sigh or a breath; if only she had tried to escape from my kisses, to defend herself, to struggle! No. She was faithful to her principles again this time, as she had always been. Her back arched docilely, her head bent under the pressure of my hand, her mouth didn't try to escape mine; her entire body went cold, inanimate, inert; she steeled herself, so to speak. Instead of a woman, I had, yet again, a corpse in my arms.

Thus, all my ardor was extinguished: chilled by my contact with that block of ice, I fled.

XVII

The day after this sad farewell, I was in Marseilles. Don't worry, dear friend, I won't be cruel enough to make you travel with me; as a matter of fact, even if I wanted to, you would probably refuse to come along. People in love make sad traveling companions: they sigh more often than they admire, and I have known some who, at a magnificent site or in a museum resplendent with masterpieces, would close their eyes in order to collect their thoughts better and meditate on their love.

From Marseilles I embarked for Italy. I visited, or rather I passed through, Rome, Naples, Florence, Venice, Milan, and Turin. Taking the coastal route in Genoa, I returned to France, three months after having left it.

I stopped in Nice; before going back to Paris, I wanted to know for sure how I was feeling and find out a little something about how Paule was feeling. Alas! I was soon sure about my own heart: the three-month absence, the dizzying race from city to city, had only made it beat faster. My imagination, which—as you know—had already been rather prone to wandering in Paris, now succumbed to reckless revelry. I had made a grave error: when one wants to calm down, to find some peace of mind, to regain control of oneself, one should not take refuge in Italy, classic land of volcanoes and secret museums.

But would this renewed wave of passion have posed a problem, if thanks to my absence, Paule's heart, living in isolation, had begun to beat like mine? What can I say? Dear friend, when one comes back from Italy, anything seems possible. Spring had recently succeeded winter, and I was counting on the April sun to dissipate the fog that had risen between my wife and me, and to melt the snow under which up to now she had been happy to live. I told myself, "Everything around her is singing of love right now; she will have to let herself be touched by that sublime harmony and will want to add her own voice to the great concert being performed by Nature." Please excuse, my friend, the poetic turn of that last sentence: I was still under the spell of Italy.

I will return to the land of prose, never to leave it again. The rest of what I have to tell you, or rather to let you guess, is not worthy of the effort of stylistic flourishes. When confronted with certain vile things, one cannot remain silent; one is obliged to speak, so as to condemn them. Indifference, disdain, or silence encourages them; the shadows that surround them give them hope for impunity; they extend, they expand, they prosper; they spread shame and dishonor all around them. They must be combatted wholeheartedly, with no fear of offending delicate ears or awakening dangerous ideas. It is because of people's ridiculous prudishness, because they thereby end up sparing vice and neglecting to stigmatize it, that vice manages, eventually, to pass itself off as virtue. If one does not dare say to a hunchback, "You have a hump," or to a dwarf, "You are deformed," that hunchback and that dwarf will go around thinking they are handsome men.

How many societies have been destroyed because they had no men strong enough or authoritative enough to cry out to them, "Take care! A new vice has just been hatched, you are being invaded by a new kind of leprosy!" Without such warning, those societies are not able to defend themselves, and the vice grows, the leprosy spreads, and does such damage that no one, having himself become vicious or leprous, takes notice anymore of the vice or leprosy of his neighbor.

Nonetheless, though it is the duty of the narrator or author to point out and stigmatize certain forms of corruption, he must do it with only a word or a stroke of the pen. He is forbidden to wallow in long descriptions and overly vivid depictions. That, dear friend, is why I was so pretentious as to tell you that I wouldn't be indulging in stylistic flourishes.

You probably haven't understood a word of this sudden digression: it is indeed a bit premature.

I pick up my story where I left off.

Upon my arrival in Nice, full of hope and enthusiasm, I wrote Paule the most touching of letters, one of those letters that are so passionate, one thinks they might make everything around them catch on fire, and one almost wonders if it's not a public safety hazard to send them through the mail.

Three days later, I received a response. She had written me by return mail, which seemed a good sign.

I locked myself in my room and read with deep concentration. She did not respond to a single word of what I had said; her letter bore no relation to mine. She told me news about her health, which had not been the best, she said, for a while. She talked about everything she had done in Paris during the winter, the fashionable plays, the concerts, and the parties that were coming up. I think she even touched on one of the political questions of the moment. She deigned, in concluding, to express the best wishes of her family and her own affection.

I must be fair to her: she had filled four pages. I had my due, I should have been satisfied, and I would have been if fate, instead of giving me the sad privilege of being her husband, had deemed it sufficient to make me her uncle. It was the kind of letter that one writes from boarding school to one's grandparents, under the watchful eye of the schoolmistress, sometimes even dictated by her.

Clearly it was pointless, for the moment, to return to Paris. I took up residence in Nice.

The hotel where I was living, the Hôtel des Princes, I think, was fairly far from the center of the city and the Promenade des Anglais. But it faced the sea and there was a wonderful view. For me, a bit fatigued from my fast-paced trip, it had above all one precious advantage: it was perfectly quiet. A Russian grande dame, too ill to make any noise, lived on the second floor; on the third, several rather well-bred Englishmen showed up from time to time; and I shared the fourth, no doubt reserved for France, with a compatriot. He was a man about forty years old, tall, a bit thin, with an appealing look about him and refined manners.

The very day after I moved into the hotel, I found myself by chance sitting next to him at the dinner table. We exchanged a few polite words at first, and then got around to talking about our travels. Like me, he had just returned from Italy, only he had stayed there for two years; before going there, he had traveled through Germany and a large part of Russia.

His conversation was as interesting as could be: he had seen everything, studied everything. He spoke of foreign rulers as if he had been received at their courts; a moment later, he was talking about the mores of the peasants of the Caucasus as if he had lived among them for a long time, intimately, so to speak.

As far as mores were concerned, I remember a discussion we had, the second time we spoke, while smoking cigars in front of the hotel, walking along the Ponchettes.

"Of all the cultures I have been able to study at my leisure," my companion said, "the French certainly have the most dissolute morals."

Since I protested, he went on: "I swear to you that only in our homeland do people let themselves be dragged into certain flights of imagination and certain aberrations. In Germany, for instance, our finely tuned forms of corruption are nearly unheard of."

"I agree with you," I answered, "that in France, among the working class, among the peasants, the morals leave something to be desired, but among the better classes of society, among the bourgeois . . ."

"That's where you are wrong," he said, interrupting me. "In our culture, only people in evening suits and silk dresses have, in a sense, the privilege of being depraved, which is logical: remember, we're not talking about physical sensation here, but only about the imagination. Luxury, idleness, and daydreaming overstimulate it and lead it to all sorts of unexpected places. The peasant and the worker don't have time to daydream; even if they did, their minds wouldn't take to it. They're too focused on concrete things to be corrupted, too naively sensual to be dissolute. They stay healthy, in fact, through the air they breathe and through the manual labor they perform; corruption is generally the result of some sort of sickly weakness. People become dissolute as they become gluttonous, as a result of a lack of appetite. Gluttons rely on new spices in order to be able to eat, the dissolute try to improve on love in order to be able to love."

My companion spoke on this topic for a long time, and I listened to him attentively. I had much to learn from such a master and especially such an observer. Throughout this story, I've often told you, dear friend (and besides, you have noticed it sufficiently on your own), that I remained naive. "Pure," I would say, if the word wasn't being used in a political sense these days. My childhood had been watched over by the most rigorous of mothers; surely, the hard work to which I devoted myself ever since and certain prudish tendencies that kept me away from dangerous friendships and easy pleasures are enough to explain my relative purity of mind. My imagination had never gone beyond certain boundaries; it was scarcely able to cross them now, in spite of the vast experience my interlocutor made available to me through his conversation. As a well-bred gentleman, he spoke, to be sure, in veiled terms, and his speech was full of tactful reticence.

XVIII

For several days we continued our conversation, but on topics with which I was more familiar and that I was able to discuss in such a way as to be interesting to my neighbor. We almost never left each other's side: at ten o'clock, we met at breakfast; we then went to take a stroll on the road to Villefranche; around three o'clock, we met again at the concert in the park where Nice society gathers; dinner found us next to each other once again; and in the evening we often ran into each other at the Foreigners' Club, in the reading room or the game room.

Despite this kind of intimacy, would you believe that I still didn't know my companion's name? I had heard him called count by the maître d' and the waiters a number of times, but with the nonchalance of the traveler who knows that even the most charming friendships have no future I had neglected to ask him what name followed that title.

One morning, I was totally enlightened on that subject; you will easily understand my surprise.

I had awakened with the presumptuous idea that the mail would bring word from Paule that day. Mail distribution time arrived, and since no one seemed to be bringing my letter to me, I told myself that it must have been put in the glass-front box used for travelers' mail and went down to the office to get it.

Naturally, I found no letter from my wife, and I was in the process of kicking myself for my naïveté, when I spied a large envelope on which I read this inscription:

> The Count de Blangy
> Hôtel des Princes
> NICE

The name Blangy, which belonged to my wife's best friend, could not possibly fail to attract my attention. At the same time, I made a connection in my mind between the word "Count" that I saw written on the envelope and the title that the hotel employees used in addressing my neighbor.

"Could his name be Blangy?" I wondered. I didn't have to wait long for an answer, since the hotel manager took the letter out from under my eyes and gave it to one of his staff, to be taken up to number 27. That was my neighbor's room.

At that point, I wondered, as you might imagine, if this count de Blangy was related to the countess.

The identical spelling of the name, the titles they both had, a number of odd little things that came back to me, some observations I had made earlier about the habits and character of my companion . . . all this soon enlightened me. In all likelihood, I had, without realizing it, formed a friendship with the husband of Paule's friend since my arrival in Nice.

Didn't everyone in society say that he had been traveling abroad for three years, and hadn't my companion expressed, the day before, his pleasure at seeing France again, after three years' absence?

Although he spoke very little about himself, hadn't he let slip, "When I was in the foreign service," and didn't I know that, shortly after his marriage, the count de Blangy had handed his letter of resignation to the minister of foreign affairs?

Finally, the way he spoke about women, and the lack of respect he seemed to have for them, confirmed his identity. This was surely the way that the man would talk who—out of fickleness, out of a taste for change—had behaved so badly toward that poor Mme de Blangy and made her a widow when she had scarcely been married. I obviously had not had the magic touch in forming my first friendship on the road.

But I soon reminded myself that the count's behavior toward his wife was none of my business. Good fortune had given me a most pleasant companion; I should be happy about it and take advantage of my discovery and the connections between us, to firm up our friendship.

"In an hour at most," I thought, strolling in front of the hotel, "we will meet at breakfast and I will hurry over to say graciously to my table mate, 'If my lucky star had not led me to meet you in Nice, I would certainly have had the pleasure of meeting you this winter in Paris; your wife and mine are best friends.'"

I had already repeated this sentence twice; I was practicing rounding it off, polishing it, when suddenly I slapped myself on the forehead, crying, "But your idea is absurd! Do you think it will be pleasant for M. de Blangy to hear you talk about his wife? He left her, he abandoned her, and you're going to remind him of his wrongdoing! He is trying his best to forget that he is married, what right do you have to make him remember it?"

Yes, good taste dictated that I should say nothing; simple social propriety demanded it. But for three months, I had not spoken about Paule to a living soul, I had not pronounced her name a single time. Here was a unique occasion for me to talk about the woman I loved so much, and I was too much in love not to yield to the temptation, even if it meant flying in the face of social propriety.

I nonetheless held out for two days; I think I would have held out even longer, if it had occurred to Paule to write me just then. I would have answered her, I would have spoken with her, and I would have thus found the strength not to talk about her. But nothing, not a single letter, not a single word; total silence, absolute muteness. So, dear friend, I was indiscreet and ridiculous. That you will see, all too well.

M. de Blangy and I were leaving the Foreigners' Club and on our way back to the hotel for dinner, when I, after wondering what the best way would be to launch into the conversation I could no longer resist starting, suddenly decided to say, "A few minutes ago, when you were reading the newspaper, I was scanning the registers where the club members sign in, and one name caught my eye."

"Which one?"

"M. de Blangy. Does this mean the count is in Nice?"

He looked at me with an astonished expression and said, "You didn't know that?"

"I had no idea. I know M. de Blangy well by reputation, but I have never actually met him."

"Are you sure?" said my interlocutor, smiling, without suspecting what was coming next.

"I am certain of it."

"Well then! Allow me to inform you that you are wrong: you have been with him constantly for the past week and he is genuinely pleased about it."

Since, to be faithful to my role, I continued to act surprised, he added, "I am the count de Blangy, I thought you knew that."

"I had no idea. I knew only one thing, that my lucky star had given me a most well-bred man, a witty and intelligent man, as my companion. That was enough for me, and I didn't think to find out his name."

"We were wrong," said the count, "not to introduce ourselves to each other, but that can be fixed."

Stopping on the sidewalk, he continued with good humor by saying, "It is my honor to introduce you to M. de Blangy."

I introduced myself as well. My name, that he had no doubt already learned by chance, didn't ring a bell for him. It was quite simple: at the time of my wedding, he had already left his wife and wasn't maintaining any contact with her.

We had just begun walking again when the count said to me, "You said that you knew a lot about me by reputation; how so?"

I was expecting that question; it was perfectly natural, and I was the one who had brought it on. But it made me uneasy nonetheless. I knew I was about to commit a blunder, but I was too far down the road to turn back.

"I have often heard about you," I answered, "from my wife."

I thought it would be more tactful to talk about my wife than his.

"So your wife knows me!"

"She met you in society before we were married."

"Really? What was her maiden name?"

"Paule Giraud."

No sooner had I spoken her name than I saw the count go pale and stumble.

But before I could make a move toward him, he had recovered and said to me, coldly, "So you married Mlle Paule Giraud. I did indeed meet her often in society, she is a beautiful woman."

That was my opinion as well, so I had nothing to respond.

We walked for a time in silence. Suddenly M. de Blangy seemed to be struggling to bring himself to say something. He stopped and said, "Does your wife still see mine?"

"Absolutely," I answered, "they're inseparable."

He cast a look at me that I will remember for the rest of my life; you would have thought that he wanted to burrow into my thoughts, to read my soul. Then he turned his head and, just as we were arriving in front of the hotel, left me abruptly, without a word, took the key to his room, and disappeared.

An hour later, the guests sat down to dinner; the count did not make an appearance.

XIX

All the next day, I didn't see him.

The day after that, we met on the Promenade des Anglais; rather than rush up to me, as he would have done two days earlier, he merely tipped his hat.

The greeting was insufficient. I had the right to be surprised, and to take offense, at such a brusque change in his manners. Between men of the better classes, the past obligates one for the future; a tipped hat does not replace a handshake from one day to the next. If I had lost M. de Blangy's esteem, he had to tell me why and I had the right to ask.

It was clear that I had displeased him by talking about his wife, but his aloofness toward me, which, given our former friendship, came very close to rudeness, was not sufficiently justified by my indiscretion.

On top of all that, the tone of his voice when he said, "So you married Mlle Paule Giraud," had struck me.

It had not been an exclamation that slipped out. I thought I had heard irony, amazement in his tone. Was there some secret between my wife and the count? Had he uncovered some mystery that I hadn't been able to figure out?

Paule had behaved so strangely toward me, had put me in such an unnatural position, that I, justifiably, suspected everything, feared everything.

I didn't waste any time making up my mind: I would see the count right away and have a frank conversation with him.

We had crossed paths, as I said, on the Promenade des Anglais, without exchanging a word. After going a few more steps, I turned. M. de Blangy seemed to be heading toward the Hôtel des Princes, by the seaside route, along the Ponchettes. I followed him at a distance. When he had entered the hotel, I gave him time to go back up to his room and settle in. Then I went up myself and knocked on the door.

"Come in," said a voice.

The key was in the door and I opened it.

"Oh, it's you, sir," said the count, unable to hide his displeasure.

"Yes, sir, it is I," I answered. "I apologize for disturbing your solitude, but I must have a moment of conversation with you. You no longer come down to meals and you seem to want to take your walks alone, so I was obliged to come knocking at your door."

"I am at your service, sir. Please be so kind as to sit down."

He offered me a chair, sat down across from me, and appeared to wait for me to explain the purpose of my visit.

"Sir," I began, in a voice that I tried to make steady but in which my emotion must have been quite apparent, "I was enjoying the pleasant relations that I had with you, from the day we met in this hotel, when suddenly those relations broke off. I don't know what the reasons were that could have made you move so brusquely from great friendliness to complete aloofness, and I've come to ask you, frankly, what they are."

"The aloofness to which you allude, sir," answered the count, "is nothing personal against you. I would ask that you please attribute it to some serious preoccupations that have suddenly overtaken me."

"If it were only a question of healing a wound to my own pride," I replied, "I would be satisfied with that response; I acknowledge that it is most appropriate. But it is not a question of my own pride here. Allow me to refresh your memory. We had spent the better part of the day together, we were chatting amiably, we had even just introduced ourselves to each other, in order to cement, as it were, our friendship, when it happened that I said my wife's maiden name. Immediately, your voice, your expression, and your manner underwent a complete metamorphosis. In front of the hotel, you took your leave of me with a curtness to which I was unaccustomed on your part; since then, you have not spoken a word to me. Please put yourself in my place for a moment. Would you not say to yourself: there is obviously some mystery there, some secret that I should know?"

"There is, sir, neither mystery nor secret."

"Do you give me your word on that?" I asked.

"But . . ."

"You hesitate? That is proof enough. I was right."

M. de Blangy wanted to protest against this rather sudden interpretation of his hesitation; I didn't give him time.

"Would you be willing, sir," I said, "to satisfy my very legitimate curiosity and help me penetrate the mystery in question?"

"Sir!" cried the count as he got up, "I repeat that there is no mystery."

"Please take note of the fact," I said, pressing my point, "that I came to you to have an entirely peaceful and courteous discussion. At this point, I am doing nothing less than begging you for that; perhaps you will agree to it if I invoke our former friendship, our pleasant conversations, and the attraction that we seemed to have to each other."

He appeared to be moved. I thought he was going to give in to my insistence. All of a sudden, he cried out, "No, no, I have nothing to say."

"That is your last word?"

"Yes, that is my last word."

"You are wrong, sir," I said firmly.

He raised his head proudly and said, "Why?"

"Oh!" I cried. "Because I am in one of those positions where one has nothing to lose, where one risks anything, where one is ready for anything, determined to do anything."

He looked at me with an expression that was more surprised than angry, and came toward me.

"Take care," he said, "you have assured me that you entered this room with peaceful intentions; in the past minute or so, your words and your tone have become almost threatening."

"I am not making threats. I am begging, fervently, a decent man to speak frankly to another man. That is your fault, count, because this scene would not be taking place if you had been more in control of yourself the other day, if you had been able to hide your feelings from me. It is your fault that I may be on the trail of a secret that I have been seeking for a long time. Well, I want to know that secret, I demand it!"

Instead of taking offense at my blunt way of expressing my wish, M. de Blangy only said, "Ah! So you've been on the trail of a secret for a long time?"

"Yes!" I cried, completely losing my head. "A secret on which my entire happiness depends. Trying to find it is draining my life away, I am as unhappy as it is possible to be ... And you, sir, who could put an end to my suffering with a single word, yes, everything has suggested as much since I walked in here, since I have been talking to you; you, who could give me some peace, refuse to explain yourself. Oh, that's cruel! I repeat, you are wrong to treat as an enemy a man reduced to despair, as I am. A man like that does not care about his life, it is just a burden for him and ..."

"And he would gladly risk it in a duel."

"Oh, yes!" I cried.

He took a step toward me and said, "So we would fight each other over your wife, is that it?"

"My wife!"

"Clearly," he said, starting to heat up as I had. "If you are unhappy, if you don't care about your life, is it not because of her? Do you really think that I haven't been able to figure out what is going on with you? Well, sir, you may have married Mlle Paule Giraud, but I married her friend. You may have been traveling away from your wife for three months, but I have been traveling for several years away from mine!"

He stopped talking, seemed to be thinking deeply, and then began again, in a calmer voice: "The way you approached me, the sincerity I read in your eyes, the half confidences that you have let slip, and the avowal of your sorrows are all, for me, proof that I am looking at an honorable man. I doubted you for a while—you will understand why later—and for that I give you my most sincere apology."

I bowed, silently, and he continued. "So you think I must know a secret, a secret that concerns you. All right then! I won't deny it. But my conscience won't allow me to tell you, unless you really push me to do so. You were talking a few minutes ago about your suffering . . . well, I need to know exactly what sort of suffering it is. Perhaps it's completely unrelated to my secret; if so, I'm warning you, I will tell you nothing. So be prepared for the fact that in that case, there'll be no use begging or threatening, it won't do any good. On the other hand, if it turns out that by telling you my secret I can in fact ease your pain, or at least give you a warning or some advice, I give you my word that I will tell you everything I know. So it is up to you, sir, to decide if I am worthy of your trust. Your secrets in exchange for mine, *if*—and I repeat *if*—I think it can be of use to you. That's my final offer."

How could I possibly hesitate, with the question phrased like that? Was this man asking to hear all my secrets not the husband of my wife's best friend, of the woman who must have been privy to all my wife's most intimate thoughts for years now? Mme de Blangy was perhaps not alone in knowing why my wife had behaved so strangely toward me; the count may well have figured the reason out himself. Before leaving his wife, had he not received Mlle Giraud in his home and observed her firsthand in that intimate setting? Was it far-fetched to think that he knew details that I did not? Pure chance had thrown me together with the only person who might be able to provide me with those details. Was I going to refuse to confide in him merely out of misplaced shame, out of some sort of exaggerated sense of scruples?

No. I spoke to him frankly, just as I am speaking to you, dear friend. I told the count about all the misadventures of my love life, sparing no detail.

He listened without saying a word, solemn and pensive. In fact, he seemed to take such an interest that it was almost as if my life story were his, that my adventures had happened to him. He made only a few comments during my story: "Yes, that's right. That's her all right! She hasn't changed a bit!"

I had just told him how curiosity and jealousy had led me to follow my wife to Rue Laffitte, and I had got to the point in my story where, suddenly seeing her leave the apartment I was watching, I ran over to the door, threw it open, and found myself face-to-face with . . .

"With Mme de Blangy!" cried the count.

"How did you guess?" I asked, shocked.

"Guess? The only thing that surprises me is that you were at all surprised. You mean you had looked around that apartment the day before and still hadn't figured it out?"

145

"But," I answered naively, "how could I have known that the ladies had rented that apartment just to visit with each other?"

The count looked at me and frowned. He has since admitted to me that, at that particular moment, he thought I might be making fun of him. My innocent expression and honest face quickly reassured him of my sincerity, however.

"Please continue," he said.

"I don't have anything important left to say," I answered. "Mme de Blangy asked me into her bachelor quarters, as she called it; Paule followed us in, and the two women proceeded to explain to me how, when I had forbidden them to see each other at home, they had been forced to start meeting at the apartment on Rue Laffitte."

"And you didn't object, you weren't outraged?" cried the count.

"God, no!" I said. "By arranging meetings with her friend, my wife was indeed guilty of not respecting my authority; but for three days, I had suspected her of such serious crimes that it did not even occur to me to complain about a simple act of disobedience like this one. Think about it, sir: I thought I was going to confront a rival, a lover, and it turned out instead that I had the great good fortune to find myself face-to-face with a charming woman from the finest of families!"

M. de Blangy moved closer to me and said, "Come now, are you serious?"

"Of course I am."

"You were actually happy to find your wife alone with mine in that apartment on Rue Laffitte?"

"I wouldn't say that I was happy, but finding them was certainly better than finding what I had thought I was going to discover."

"Well, sir! All I can say is that I do not agree with you. Personally, I would have preferred to be in a position to get my revenge."

"Revenge is a good thing," I replied, "and I assure you that I have thought about it more than once. But I hope you will agree that it's much more pleasant to be able to say, 'I thought my wife was unfaithful to me, but she is not: my wife is not guilty.'"

These last few words, spoken in total innocence, were a revelation for M. de Blangy. He could no longer doubt that I was utterly naive.

XX

Indeed, my naïveté was so complete that the count had a very hard time making me see the light. My mind rebelled and prevented me from believing what I was hearing, at least for a while. Some minds work like that, my dear friend: they have great difficulty truly taking in certain thoughts. In spite of an inherent decency that had always made me shy away from prurient stories and an exceptional life that had always sheltered me from dangerous sights, I did have some awareness of life's miseries. But I had always honestly believed that a good family and a proper education acted as impenetrable barriers between certain social classes and those ills.

M. de Blangy was willing to concede that such things existed only as exceptions to the rule in the better classes of society, but I refused to believe in even those exceptions.

I was nonetheless forced to admit, eventually, what was all too obvious.

Seduced by the dazzling beauty of Paule's friend, by her wit and originality, the count had made, as I had, a love match. But he was less at fault than I had been: far from sharing Mlle Giraud's frankness, M. de Blangy's fiancée had done nothing whatsoever to dissuade him from marrying her. On the contrary, she put to work all the seductive qualities Nature had granted her, in order to convince him to give her his name and his fortune. It is true—it's only fair to give her credit for this—that she absolutely did not behave with M. de Blangy the way Paule behaved with me; she put no bolt on the door and did not appear to have taken any vows of chastity. The count had one incontestable advantage over me: he had been a husband to his wife. But it did not take him long to notice her coldness, her distance, and the repugnance she felt in fulfilling her wifely duties. She brought to their relationship such aloofness, such total indifference, that M. de Blangy, who had become accustomed, before his marriage, to finding women more willing and uninhibited, became seriously alarmed. Just as I had, one day he wondered if Mme de Blangy wasn't being parsimonious in her marriage only in order to be guiltily generous elsewhere. He followed her, saw her go into a building on Rue Louis-le-Grand, bribed the concierge, managed to hide in the apartment, and, more skillful than I, was able to hear a conversation between his wife and the woman who was (alas!) destined to become mine later on.

The content of that conversation, in which marriage was shamelessly disparaged, was so offensive to the count that he didn't hesitate to intervene.

He made his appearance at the very moment they were saying the worst things about him. Paule, as a young girl would, blushed, went pale, and ended up having a nervous fit. As far as the countess was concerned, she pushed audacity to its limit: she retracted nothing of what M. de Blangy had just heard, and was brazen enough to go so far as to glorify herself, in a sense, for having such subversive ideas.

During the rather dissipated life he had led before his marriage, the count had sometimes heard strange theories argued, but even so he was astounded, devastated. Indignation turned to stupor, anger to contempt; he didn't know how to respond and no longer had the strength to punish.

Punish! How could he?

"The law," he told me, "would obviously have refused me any help; lawmakers have failed to foresee certain misdeeds, which are thus granted impunity. I could barely obtain a separation from the courts: Mme de Blangy's wrongdoings toward me were of such a nature that judges often refuse to admit them as evidence, so that they won't have to punish them. And what proof could I have given of these deeds? Whose testimony could I have called on? Mlle Paule Giraud's? She would have been far too interested a party in the debate for her word to be taken into consideration; and she would have died rather than compromise her friend. Come now, I know her well! She's an indomitable creature that only my wife has been able to find the secret of dominating. Was I supposed to act on my own? Ah! Sir, men of society have nowhere to turn in cases like this. Brutality and violence repulse them. They shrink from the rumors that would spring up around their names; they're afraid of ridicule. How would I have escaped ridicule? I've seen my fellow club members make merciless fun of poor husbands cheated on in ordinary conditions; would they have seen fit to spare me because of the odd and completely exceptional position in which I found myself? No, they would have laughed at me, without even stopping to think about placing blame on Mme de Blangy. In this nineteenth-century Parisian society of ours, people enjoy, either out of frivolity or a love of paradox, jeering at the victims and absolving the guilty parties. That is how vices of all sorts, sure of impunity, often sure of protection even, insinuate themselves into our mores."

I admit, dear friend, that I was barely listening at that point to M. de Blangy's recriminations against contemporary society. Only the confidences he had just made to me were on my mind.

"But you at least," I said in a moment of lucidity, "forbade them from seeing each other again. You tried to keep them away from each other, did you not?"

"Certainly I tried," M. de Blangy cried. "But do you think that a man with any self-respect at all can play the role of spy and his wife's jailer for very long? The constant surveillance fatigues you, sickens you, and wears away, over time, even the firmest will, the most galvanized energy."

"Who was stopping you," I replied, "from forcing your wife to come with you on your travels? Once you were abroad, surveillance would have become unnecessary."

"That is where you are wrong! The first day I left her alone for a minute, in the hotel, she would have raced like the wind to the next means of transportation leaving for Paris and would not have wasted a minute in meeting up again with her inseparable friend."

"But what if," I cried emphatically, "Mme de Blangy didn't know how to find that friend in Paris? If, while you were dragging your wife off on your travels, Mlle Giraud herself was suddenly wrenched away from Rue Caumartin? If, while you were taking one off in the direction of America, for example, someone took the other off in the direction of Russia, without warning either of them or letting them know the itinerary to be followed? Where would they find each other? When would they see each other again?"

I stopped to appreciate the effect that my idea was surely producing on the count.

"But who in the world," he said, "would have had the will and the power to wrench Mlle Giraud away from Paris, and make her travel all over the globe against her will, for an unlimited amount of time? Neither her father nor her mother, that's for sure."

Entrenched in my idea, I interrupted, crying, "I am not talking about what you might have done in the past, count, but rather about what you could do right now. Since the Code requires Mme de Blangy to follow you wherever it pleases you to take her, since it offers you the means to oblige her to do so, does it not give me, every bit as married as you are, the same rights over Mlle Giraud? She's not a minor anymore, dependent on her family, but a married woman, dependent on me alone.

"Nothing would prevent us," I continued animatedly, "from leaving this evening or tomorrow for Paris. We go to a hotel in order to keep our arrival secret; we make preparations for a long trip, in haste and in secret; we cash in, if necessary, some bonds so as not to be stopped on the road by some wretched money problem; if need be, we go to court and get an audience with the magistrate, who gives us the legal means to make our wives obey us. Come now, sir, it is no longer a matter of tact and sensibilities. The law protects us, let us use it! Once the preparations are finished and all the formalities fulfilled, we shake hands and bid each other farewell. Two carriages take us to Rue Caumartin; one stops at your door, the other at mine. We go upstairs, and without giving the women the time to see each other, to write to each other, to give each other a sign, we drag them off. They may well resist; well, sir, aren't we resolved to do everything necessary, haven't we foreseen everything? We use force if necessary to oblige them to follow us, and, the day after our raid on our respective households, carried away by two express trains moving in opposite directions, we find ourselves more than two hundred miles away from each other . . . What do you say about my plan?"

"It just might work."

"Indeed."

"But," said the count, after a moment of reflection, "while you have been separated from your wife for barely four months, I have been separated from mine for more than three years. Your misfortune is quite recent, so your wounds are still open, whereas mine healed a long time ago. In the past, I might have accepted your proposition enthusiastically. At this point, I decline because I am no longer in love."

"No longer in love!" I cried. "Then why do you persist in your voluntary exile, why did you not return a long time ago to Paris, where everything—your tastes, your habits, your career, your friends—beckons you? Why vegetate here when you could be living up there?"

He hung his head and didn't answer. Emboldened by this initial success, I continued: "All right then! I will concede that you are no longer in love. Scorn has killed love for both of us. We have become totally indifferent to our wives. They are not worth the trouble that it would take to get them back. But what about morality, the same morality you were invoking a few minutes ago? You were indignantly deploring the people who cannot bring themselves to condemn and punish certain misdeeds. But the people you were talking about don't have an interest, as we do, in such repression. Will you reserve all your anger for other people and grant yourself a full pardon? No, sir, no; we owe it to society, we owe it to ourselves, to challenge reprehensible aberrations!"

I spoke for a long time like this. My dear friend, I was no longer the young husband you knew, full of tact and reserve, innocent and prudish, spending his life wanting only to become a cipher. The light had shone through! I knew, I saw, and I wanted!

XXI

Three days after that conversation, I arrived in Paris, accompanied by the count, and went to a hotel on Rue du Bac. We had thought it wise to put the Seine between us and our wives, so as not to run the risk of a chance encounter. All our errands would be run by carriage, and we had made up our minds to beg for the discretion of the people we would need to see.

We each deployed such energy in our purchases, our transfers of funds, and our various procedures, that forty-eight hours after our arrival in Paris we were ready to leave again and in a position to oblige our wives to follow us.

"So will it be tonight?" I asked the count, meeting him at the hotel around four in the afternoon.

"Tonight for certain. Nothing is holding us back at this point and I am eager to get it over with. What route do you plan to take, so that I can choose a different one? That is an important point to discuss."

"Please decide on your itinerary, and I will set mine accordingly."

"Unless you see any reason why not," responded the count, "I will go north: I will forge straight ahead, but I cannot tell you the exact stops I will make."

"I don't need to know what they are. You have chosen north. I choose south. I will take, this very evening, the express train to Marseilles, or perhaps the one to Bordeaux, it doesn't matter."

"So you will have to be at one of those two stations by eight o'clock."

"I will be there."

"In that case, all that is left for us to do is say good-bye, wish each other luck, and head for Rue Caumartin."

"It would seem so."

We immediately had our two carriages pulled up, our trunks brought down, and we took leave of each other.

We shook hands warmly; over the past several days, we had come to feel both affection and respect for each other.

At six in the evening, my carriage stopped on Rue Caumartin, in front of my house. I got out immediately and, without asking the concierge for any information, climbed the stairs, opened the door to my apartment (to which I had a key), and went into the drawing room.

My heart was beating fast enough to explode, but I was calm in appearance and resolute.

Paule, sitting in a chair with a book in her lap, cried out with surprise when she saw me, then got up and came over to greet me, holding out her hand.

I did not hold out mine.

"Well!" she said with astonishment. "After four months of separation, you don't even say hello to me?"

I looked at her and did not respond.

She had visibly changed since I saw her last: her fresh coloring had disappeared; the blood seemed to have been drained from her lips, lips that had always been so crimson. A sort of excavation had been hollowed out around her eyes, and large bluish circles surrounded them. Her figure had gotten slimmer, and despite the loose clothes that covered her there was no mistaking how very thin her entire body was.

"Why are you looking at me like that?" she asked me.

"I find you much changed," I answered.

"That's possible. I have been suffering for some time now from neuralgia and heart palpitations. From nerves, no doubt. But what a strange way you have of greeting me!"

"I begin by asking about your health; isn't that the natural thing to do? You must take care of yourself."

"Go ahead and dictate your prescription," she said, smiling, "since it seems that it is a doctor who has come back to me."

"You must," I continued, "have a change of scenery, travel, take exercise."

"Really? I will consider that prescription, doctor, and perhaps one day I will follow your advice."

"No, you must follow it today."

"What do you mean, today?"

"Yes, you have an hour to get ready to leave."

At the same time, without looking at her, without appearing to notice her astonishment, I walked to the fireplace and pulled the bell cord.

A chambermaid appeared.

"Madame," I said to the girl, "is leaving, tonight, on a trip. Put all her most indispensable personal items in a trunk. She will be along in a minute to help you. Go on now, and hurry."

"But, sir, you are mad!" Paule cried, when the chambermaid had left the room.

"I have never been more sane," I replied.

"And you think that I will leave like this, all of a sudden, to obey some arbitrary caprice?"

"Oh, it's not a caprice, it is my firm and unshakable will."

"So this is not about my health. Even if it happens that I am sick, you had no way of knowing that."

"I knew you were gravely ill morally; that was enough for me. I have just discovered that you are physically ill as well, and I am all the more determined to put my plans into action."

"What are they? I only know them in part."

"No, you know them in their entirety: you are leaving Paris, this evening, at eight o'clock."

"Really? And I am leaving by myself?"

"No, I am accompanying you."

"Well then! It's no longer enough for you to travel, now you must make other people travel too."

"That's well put."

"And where are you taking me?"

"I have no idea."

"Delightful!" she cried and burst out laughing.

I didn't bat an eye, and when the fit of nervous laughter was over, I began again, with the greatest calm: "Allow me to bring to your attention the fact that the clock is ticking. If you do not give your chambermaid instructions, she will pack your trunks all wrong, and tomorrow, after a night on the train, when you arrive at the hotel, none of the things you need will be there."

"I have no instructions to give," she said, sitting down. "I am not leaving."

"I beg your pardon," I replied. "You are leaving, by fair means or foul."

"Foul!" she cried.

"All right then, foul. I have taken all the precautions. Look at this," I said, taking a piece of paper from my pocket. "All I have to do is send this letter right around the corner, to M. Bellanger, who is officially advised here to put himself at my disposal. Perhaps you do not know M. Bellanger; he is nonetheless well known around the neighborhood. Believe me, you do not want to force me to bother him; just come along willingly."

She looked at me, thought for a moment, grasped the seriousness of the situation, and suddenly made up her mind: "We will travel then, so be it! You demand it, and the law gives you rights over me. But I won't be able to leave this evening. I have good-byes to say."

"To whom?" I asked.

"My mother and father."

"They will be here in just a minute. I had them advised of your departure. To whom else do you wish to say good-bye?"

"To Mme de Blangy."

"I expected that," I said, losing a bit of my calm. "Well, Mme de Blangy has no time to listen to your good-byes; she is leaving, like you, on a trip this very evening."

"Berthe! That's impossible," she cried. "You're lying to me."

"Why wouldn't she be leaving? You are."

"First of all, no, I am not leaving. Besides that, she doesn't have, as I do, the misfortune of being under a husband's control."

"Really? So the count is dead?"

"More or less, since she doesn't know what has become of him."

"I will tell you what has become of him. He is, at this very moment, just a few steps away from us, on Rue Caumartin, on the third floor, in his home. He is announcing to his wife plans exactly like mine. He is expressing his will to her; if she refuses to submit, he says, 'Nothing, nothing, do you hear me, neither scandal nor violence, will make me back down. You will come with me, I demand that you come with me.' And she will go with him, because one doesn't resist a man as determined as M. de Blangy, a man who has terrible weapons he could use against his wife and against you!"

She went pale and hung her head.

I continued, becoming more and more animated, "You do understand what I am saying, don't you? I met M. de Blangy in Nice, I became friendly with him, and we confided in each other. I know how much influence the countess has over you, and I swore that I would extract you from that influence. M. de Blangy took an oath to back me up, and we are men of our word. Come on now! Get up and get ready to come with me."

Astounded, devastated, unsure of a course of action, she remained seated.

All of a sudden, I heard the doorbell. Going over to her, I said, "It's your mother, come to tell you good-bye. No recriminations, I beg you, and no complaints, or else I will complain too; I will explain why I am forced to drag you away from Paris."

"Oh!" she cried, getting up. "You wouldn't, would you?"

"I told you that I would not hesitate to do anything, anything at all, do you understand? You must come with me right away. If you hesitate one more minute, I will speak, and having spoken, I will act."

"Very well," she said, in a very low voice, "I will come with you."

M. and Mme Giraud entered. I took care of explaining their daughter's sudden departure: a relative of mine in the provinces was very ill, I had just spent several days with him, and he had pleaded with me to bring my wife to him as quickly as possible; he wanted to see her before he died.

Paule confirmed this tale, kissed her father and mother, promised to come back soon, and went into her dressing room.

I followed her; the count and I had agreed that until the time of departure we would not leave our wives' sides for a single minute. We had to prevent them from writing to each other, at any cost.

Paule, who seemed resigned, gave orders to her chambermaid in front of me, and hurriedly took from her wardrobe various objects that she put into an overnight bag. She then threw a shawl around her shoulders and, covering her head with a little traveling cap, said, "I am at your service."

She went downstairs, and I followed her, watching her every movement.

My carriage was waiting in the street. I opened the door and helped Paule get in. Since, having cast a glance all around, I saw no one on the sidewalk, I thought it was safe to go have a word with my servant, who was helping the coachman load the trunks on the carriage.

When I turned around a minute later, I saw a woman in a bonnet quickly crossing the sidewalk. I recognized her: she was Mme de Blangy's chambermaid. While I had been watching the sidewalk, she had approached in the middle of the street, Paule had leaned out the door, and they had had time to exchange a few words.

What could they have said to each other? It was pointless to ask my wife about it. I got into the carriage and cried out to the coachman, so that everyone could hear, "To Montparnasse Station!" The carriage took off at a trot in the direction of the boulevard. Going down Rue Caumartin, we crossed paths with a carriage that was coming up the street: I thought I recognized it as the one that had taken the count to his wife's house, two hours earlier. Our double expedition had succeeded.

On Rue de Rivoli, I leaned out the door and changed the itinerary I had originally given to the coachman.

A few minutes before eight o'clock we were pulling up to Lyons Station. I bought two tickets to Marseilles, and we boarded the express train.

XXII

My conversation with Paule, from Paris to Marseilles, was not, as I am sure you can easily understand, dear friend, among the most animated. The situation between us was too tense for us to even consider chatting about banalities. As far as going back to the discussion we had been having when M. and Mme Giraud arrived, I did not dream of it. I had said to Paule all that I had to say; she knew that I was aware of her behavior, and I had not hidden the indignation it provoked in me. But I was not the type of man to wage constant war on her, to assail her with the weapons M. de Blangy's revelations had put in my hands, to crush her with limitless anger. My love had survived the blows it had suffered; I became, in a sense, an accomplice to my wife's misdeeds. It would have been ungracious of me to reproach her for them, and the scorn I would have made her feel would have come back, to some extent, to haunt me.

So I made up my mind, out of self-respect, not to talk about the past anymore, to forget it as much as possible and to make a new life for myself, as well as for Paule. You may accuse me of being a bit too indulgent and quick to forgive, but I would respond that you are in no position to judge my case. I was not indulgent, I was in love; that is my only excuse. How could my love live on? Ah, that is what may astonish you and what you have a right to reproach me for. But your astonishment can never be as great as mine; in terms of reproaches, I spare myself none.

Do not think, however, that I was disposed to give my love free rein, to lavish it once again on the woman who inspired it, or to make use of the situation created by the rigorous measures I had decided to take. No, I would be able to control myself, I would be able to wait; wasn't I used to it? Despite my culpable attachment to her, I still had some sense of dignity; it would not have been fitting for me, from one day to the next, to confess my weakness to Paule, and to consent, without transition, to succeed . . . the person who had preceded me. I wanted her imagination to have the time to calm down, I wanted a sort of peace to come over her, for her to understand her mistakes and be ashamed of them. Having been prey for several years to pernicious advice and dangerous examples, having been bent under an infernal domination, unaware of her wrongdoing, intoxicated, blinded, crazed, she needed to come back to freedom slowly, to regain her independence. Light had to shine into her mind and into her heart. Hers was a soul to be saved: well then, save it I would! And if you find me ridiculous, so much the worse for you.

Thanks to the *express* trains and especially to the *rapides*, there is no longer any distance at all between Paris and Marseilles. My intention was therefore not to stay in Marseilles, where I would have had to exercise constant surveillance over Paule in order to keep her from going back to Rue Caumartin. I had decided to continue my travels and embark on one of the first steamships leaving the port.

If M. de Blangy had dragged his wife north, that is to say to England, as he had said he planned to, both the English Channel and the Mediterranean would separate the two friends, and I could, without presuming too much, begin to hope again.

When we arrived at the station in Marseilles, instead of going to a hotel I took a carriage; I helped Paule get in and ordered the coachman to take us to the port.

A ship was blowing steam near the pier. I obtained the necessary information: the ship, headed for Oran, was supposed to leave at five o'clock (it was a Wednesday) and arrive Friday night or Saturday morning.

I went back to my wife.

"If you agree," I said, pointing out the vessel, "we will sail on that ship."

"I don't have to agree," she replied. "Do with me whatever you wish."

She got out, took my arm, and soon we were settled on board, with all our luggage.

After an excellent crossing, we debarked in the port of Oran Saturday morning and had ourselves taken to Place Kléber, to the Hôtel de la Paix, where we found very comfortable accommodations, composed of two bedrooms separated by a large drawing room.

You see, dear friend, I was not taking advantage of the situation. I had resigned myself to living as a bachelor on the African coast, just as I had in Paris. Although I had put two oceans between Paule and Mme de Blangy, I was also discreet enough, at least for the moment, to put the thickness of several walls between my wife and me.

I will give you as few details as possible about my stay in Oran. In my state of mind, I paid very little attention to the city to which chance had led me, and to its inhabitants.

I had but one thought: distract my wife, redirect her thoughts, erase the past from her memory, help her develop a taste for a new life, and, finally, please her.

This was not an easy task, I assure you. Not that Paule obstinately refused, as I had feared, to engage in any outing or pleasurable activity. She had nothing against such things. She did not even seem to hold a grudge against me for the violent way I had dealt with her, and I realized, on several occasions, that none of my tactfulness went unnoticed and that she was grateful for the care I took. But she was, most of the time, deep in a sort of prostration that was very difficult to overcome, despite real and visible efforts on her part.

At first I thought that she was only morally ill and that she was suffering from the too sudden changes that had taken place in her life. But soon I thought I was seeing physical signs, signs that her health had been completely perturbed. The loss of weight I had already noticed upon my return to Paris progressed each day; her eyes were starting to shine, her pupils to dilate; she complained of palpitations, of shortness of breath every time she walked a bit too fast, of violent pain in her head and in her chest, of a dry little cough that I often heard at night, from my room; finally, she was constantly subject to a host of nervous phenomena and episodes, caused, without a doubt, by a general weakening of her system.

She was perfectly aware of her state and seemed to be worried about it. I proposed that she go see a doctor. She agreed to.

Doctor X, with whom I quickly made contact, had practiced for years in Paris and was renowned among his colleagues, when he was forced to abandon his many patients and settle in Africa, for health reasons. More or less cured for two years, Doctor X had stayed in Oran out of gratitude, had married there, and practiced medicine there, to the great joy of the French colonists, who found themselves being cared for just as they would have been in Paris.

I rushed to get my wife to the doctor. He examined her for a long time, seemed to study her with extreme care, and, without making any pronouncement about the nature of her ailment, did nothing but write her a prescription.

But, when I was taking my leave of him, he let me know that he would like to see me.

An hour later, he and I were alone in his office.

"Your wife's condition is fairly serious," he said. "I feel it my duty to inform you of that."

"What is the name of her disease?" I asked, upset.

"For the moment, she does not have an actual disease, but she is in a state of chloroanemia that must be vigorously combatted."

"Let us combat it then, doctor; thanks to you, I have no doubt we will win the battle."

"You are wrong to look at it that way. There is not much I can do, but you can do everything."

"Me!"

"Yes, you. Would you allow me to ask you a few questions, even though you aren't the patient?"

"Go ahead, doctor."

"What kind of life did you lead as a young man?"

"The most laborious and least dissipated kind of life."

"I thought so. You did not live like a lowlife, as they have started saying in Paris since I left. You did not squander your health. You kept yourself fresh and in good shape, and then, in the prime of life, you married the woman of your choice, and a very pretty woman at that, my goodness! How long have you been married?"

"Soon it will be a year," I replied sadly.

"I thought so. You are newlyweds."

The conversation was starting to aggravate me.

"What conclusion do you draw from my answers, doctor?" I asked.

"Oh, you understand what I'm getting at," he said. "When one is young, passionate, and in love, one simply doesn't realize, one doesn't stop to think that certain feminine dispositions need care, need to be treated gently. You see, dear sir, young women raised in big cities, as your wife was, that is to say in a hothouse, deprived of sun and fresh air, should never be loved too passionately. Although passion charms them, it also kills them, because they're not prepared for it. A husband, in certain cases, needs to know how to moderate his excitement and exercise some control over his desires."

"So according to you," I said, smiling bitterly, "I have failed to control my desires?"

"The examination that I have just given your wife certainly seems to suggest that. I'm not saying you committed any crime. You sinned out of ignorance. But please, take this as a warning, stop being selfish."

To think that these things were being said to me! Me! I was being accused of having lacked consideration for my wife!

I promised the doctor not to be selfish anymore. What else could I say? I had no desire to expose all my sorrows to him.

"At least," I added, "can you promise me that you will cure your new patient?"

"I hope so, if the cause of the illness goes away. But don't forget, her condition is serious, and could lead to cerebral complications. If we are not careful, we are very slowly headed for what they called in my day diffuse perimeningoencephalitis, and what they call these days simply pachymeningitis."

These excessively technical terms did nothing to reassure me or cheer me up. I took my leave of the doctor, fearing that once he got started, he wouldn't stop. Wasn't I sufficiently well enlightened about Paule's state? Thanks to the trip that was under way, I would be her savior, physically as well as morally.

XXIII

Aside from the personal recommendations given to me by Doctor X, which were easy enough to follow, the treatment prescribed for Paule was very simple. She needed to get lots of exercise, spend time in the fresh air, and enjoy herself as much as possible.

Thus, nothing kept us in Oran and prevented me from following to the letter the plan that M. de Blangy and I had mapped out, consisting of a policy of not staying more than one week in the same city. I took Paule on some interesting excursions, on the coast and inland, and I took away any opportunity, in case she was considering it, for her to send news back to France and especially for her to receive letters. But on our second visit to the doctor, it occurred to him to recommend that my wife try the efficacy of the hot springs three kilometers outside Oran, known as the Bains de la Reine, named in commemoration of the marvelous treatment that Princess Jeanne, daughter of Queen Isabella, had undergone there in the time of the Spanish domination.

So we settled, so to speak, in Oran. I rented a carriage to take us every morning to the baths and employed a little Arab boy, twelve or thirteen years old, with an intelligent face, who went by the name Ben-Kader: a *yaouley*, as they call them down there.

We spent our time very pleasantly. From the Bains de la Reine, we would go eat lunch in Saint-André, a picturesque seaside village, and after resting for an hour or two we usually climbed up to the little city of Mers-el-Kébir, at the summit of which is a famous fortress with a magnificent view. Sometimes, leaving the springs, we would return to Oran by the most direct route; then we would spend the afternoon making excursions within the city, especially to the Promenade de Létang, where the entire horizon is taken up by the immensity of the Mediterranean.

Ben-Kader always followed us, was always ready to help and to provide us with information in the patois the little Arabs use to make themselves understood by the French.

"You know, you, sir," he would say to me sometimes, when he saw that I was looking for Paule, "the lady, she went there, in the street."

The fact is that Ben-Kader had a much better idea of what was going on in the street and on the public square than inside the hotel, a place he entered only with great reluctance.

The *yaouley* have an instinctive horror of the interior walls and ceilings of a building. They need fresh air, open space, blue sky overhead. Barefoot, barely covered by baggy pants and a calico jacket cinched at the waist by a red belt, their heads covered by a red fez, they mainly sit on the sidewalks next to public squares or busy streets and take care of horses.

As soon as an officer sets foot on the ground, at the door of a café, a crowd of *yaouley* rushes toward him. He usually recognizes his favorite and confers upon him the care of his horse. Instead of taking the horse's bridle, the little Arab immediately sits down in front of the horse and starts talking to him. The animal, used to this way of doing things, waits patiently for his master for several hours, in the company of his caretaker. When the horseman comes back, the *yaouley*, still sitting down, cries out to him, "You know, sir, you give me two sous."

The coins are tossed to him, and he is delighted: he has earned his day's wages.

Did Paule often give two sous to Ben-Kader or had she just somehow figured out how to win him over? What I do know for sure is that he obeyed her much better than he did me and that he appeared to be completely devoted to her.

After dinner, I would ordinarily spend a half hour at the Café Soubiran, then I would meet my wife in the drawing room between our two bedrooms. While she busied herself with embroidery work, I would read to her some good book or other that I had procured with her in mind. The evening drifted by like this, and by ten o'clock we had retired to our respective rooms. This life—active all day and intellectual at night, free of all worry—had a positive effect on Paule's health. Her strength was coming back, her color was slowly improving, and she was getting plump again, as she had been when I first knew her.

As far as her character was concerned, she also seemed to be making progress. I had promised myself, out of tact, you know, never to reproach her about her behavior toward me and never to talk about the past. But during our reading, occasionally a line or a word would remind us of our situation and seem to allude to it. At those moments, Paule, who would not have been perturbed at all in the old days, blushed and hung her head.

One day, she even risked making a few comments that I cannot keep to myself. We were reading the first few pages of a novel, in which the author, after having told of his heroine's childhood, began to talk about her youth and the education planned for her.

"As long as they don't send her to the convent!" Paule cried suddenly.

This observation stopped me short in my reading and I said, "You think that the convent is dangerous for a young girl?"

"It can be," she answered.

"What kind of education do you think is better?"

"The kind one receives from one's mother, at home."

"It isn't always easy for a mother to raise her daughter well."

"Well then, she should raise her badly, but she should raise her herself: even if the intellectual training falls short, at least she will have given her daughter a sense of decency."

"You don't approve of boarding schools at all?"

"I approve of small boarding schools with a maximum of forty students or so."

"Why?"

"Because you can keep a close eye, a sort of maternal eye, on the students. It's not the religious education that takes place in convents that I object to. (Heaven forbid! I would hate to be a freethinker.) It's the fact that they are open to three or four hundred girls of all ages and of all conditions. The younger ones are separated from the older ones, people argue. In the first place, that's not entirely accurate; there are many circumstances in which they come together and speak with each other. Aside from that, how do you define 'younger' and 'older'? The ones who are ten to thirteen years old and the ones who are between fifteen and seventeen, that's how the convents usually group them, and it's absurd: at thirteen, some girls are, morally speaking, grown up; on the other hand, many seventeen-year-olds deserve to be still among the younger ones. The convents group by physical criteria, in the traditional way, when in order to be prudent, they need to use a moral classification. So what happens? The innocent ones come into constant contact with those who are no longer innocent and soon lose their naïveté and the virginity of their souls. In a small school, the headmistress and the schoolmistresses live with their students, as in a family. They chat with them, listen to their secrets, know their faults, and can lead the dangerous sheep away from the flock. If they are respectable women, they have a good influence over all those young hearts. In the convent, the nuns are probably motivated by excellent intentions, but their influence is too diffuse to be useful. They give the children their lessons, but they do not give them advice. And then too, those women are generally too saintly to make really good schoolteachers: they don't know about evil and refuse to believe in it. They are ignorant about a whole host of little details concerning communal living among women, details it would behoove them to know."

She stopped. I said to her, "So you don't think that a young girl raised in the convent can turn out to be a respectable woman?"

"My Lord!" she cried. "I am far from thinking such a thing. The impressions made in the convent certainly fade away; even the most impressionable students can turn out to be successful wives and excellent mothers."

"But can some of them escape the bad influences you are talking about altogether and leave the convent as pure as they entered it?"

"Certainly," she replied. "It's a matter of chance; it depends on which of their classmates they spent time with."

The turn that our conversation was taking must have brought back some old memories for her. With her elbow on the table and her head in her hand, she remained silent for a moment. Suddenly, without changing position, her eyes downcast, she said in a voice full of emotion, as if she were talking to herself, "You are fourteen years old and your mind is already aware of things (but only flirtatious things, a sort of instinctive feminine flirtatiousness); it is pure of anything dirty, thanks to the education you have received from your mother up to that point. Suddenly, you go off to boarding school. A chill comes over you, a feeling of solitude creeps in, you feel lost among all these girls whom you do not know and who stare at you without saying a word; at recess, you run and hide in a corner, to daydream about the little room where you were so happy, the house where you spent so many happy days, and all the people who live there. 'Oh, how sad my mother must be!' you tell yourself. 'I'm sure she's crying this very moment.'

And you cry yourself, at the memory of the tears she shed, so recently, as she tore herself away from your arms.

"When you lift your head, you see that you are no longer alone on the bench where you sought refuge. A young girl about your age is sitting next to you; she takes your hand, without any objection on your part, and says, 'Don't cry, you won't be unhappy here; we have fun sometimes, you'll see. Where are you from? Have you ever been away at school before?'

"You answer, all too happy to have someone with whom to chat and exchange secrets.

"Little by little, you become attached and you end up loving with all your heart the girl who first showed you a bit of sympathy, when all the others were still treating you like a stranger. It is so easy to win a fourteen-year-old heart! It gives itself with such abandon and is so delighted to do so! If it were a man who said, 'What a lovely waist you have! I adore your eyes, your hands are charming, let me admire them!,' you would blush instinctively, you would run away at once, so as not to hear such things. But it is a woman speaking, a young girl like you; you listen to her without letting it bother you, often with pleasure, and you return her compliments.

"As one compliment leads to another and one secret leads to another, your companion begins to have an influence over you. She has been in the convent for several years, you have been there for only a month or two; she knows all the ins and outs and teaches them to you. She is also more fully developed, more formed, more experienced than you; she puts her experience at your service, and since you are at an age where you want nothing more than to learn, you listen to her.

"Soon it is no longer just affection that you have for her, it is fear and respect. You feel ignorant and small next to her. She has managed, by winning a bit more of your confidence every day, by worming her way into your life, by exercising over your mind a sort of slow and continuous pressure, to force you to see only through her eyes, to take away your sense of right and wrong, to dominate you, to subjugate you to her whims.

"Sometimes you try to remove the shackles, but you cannot: a thousand indissoluble bonds, a thousand tyrannical memories link you to each other, until you leave the convent. It's only then that the links break, that the memories fade . . . unless," she added, lowering her voice, "chance, or rather fate, brings you together again, and at that point . . ."

"At that point?" I asked.

"At that point," she murmured, "you are lost."

"What!" I cried. "You don't think that someone can escape from the kind of domination you're talking about?"

"Of course!" she said. "With the help of time and distance."

After a moment, she added, as if she wanted to conclude, "More often than not, I'm convinced, men don't ruin women, women ruin each other."

You see, dear friend, she had come, on her own, without any reproach or moralizing on my part, to judge her past life and to condemn it.

I assure you that she spoke in all sincerity, with no intention of inspiring a confidence in me of which she could take advantage later or of trying to make me have a higher opinion of her. She had genuinely headed down a new path, with that liveliness, that boldness, that sort of relative frankness you must have already seen in her, if I have done a decent job of depicting her character. Nonetheless, as she herself admitted, only time could keep her on that path, strengthen her in her resolutions, erase from her mind those early impressions, and close her mind completely to the influences that had so long been exercised over her.

Alas, I was too happy about the results gained so far to worry about the future; time would be on my side, I had no doubt. What event, what accident could disturb the progress that was taking place? Wasn't the site of our retreat unknown to everyone? Did Paule herself have the vaguest notion of the whereabouts of the woman who alone had enough power over her mind to lead her astray?

Full of confidence in a better destiny, convinced that my fate depended on me, and that my dreams, so long cherished, were about to come true, I was not nervous and impatient as I had been in the past; my love was calmer. It had metamorphosed: I was beginning to see Paule as nothing but a sick child, whom I was responsible for raising and curing.

I had come to love my task, as a doctor comes to love the patient declared terminal by his colleagues and whom he hopes to save, as the chaplain of a prison grows attached to the criminal who has been won over by his sermons and touched by repentance. My love was becoming metaphysical; I felt less desire and more tenderness.

Paule seemed to be deeply moved by my care and my tact. She often thanked me with a smile, a look, or a squeeze of my hand. I even thought I noticed her becoming a little flirtatious with me, probably for the sake of contrast.

You see, dear friend, I am nearing the finish line and you have no doubt that I will cross it. I thank you for that vote of confidence, but before you start celebrating on my behalf, please turn the page of this manuscript.

XXIV

In Oran, I developed the habit of getting up early in the morning and taking a fairly long ride on horseback, while Paule was still asleep or dressing. Ben-Kader watched for me to return, and as soon as he saw me reach the public square, he went off to tell my wife. She would come down right away, and we would get into the carriage that came to pick us up, every day at ten, to take us to the Bains de la Reine.

One morning, it was a Saturday, I think, when I stopped in front of the hotel, Ben-Kader walked over to me and stood in front of my horse. "You know, you," he said to me, in a sad voice, "the lady, she is gone."

"What lady?" I asked, not understanding.

"Your lady."

"Gone where?" I said, stepping to the ground.

He stretched his arm out toward the ocean in a solemn gesture and said, "There."

I could not prevent a shudder, but pulled myself together immediately. Had I not just that very day seen Paule before I got on my horse and had she not told me to come back as soon as I could? Tired of waiting for me, she had probably gone for a walk in the direction of the port; that's what the *yaouley* meant.

I went into the hotel. Seeing a bellboy, I asked, without giving any particular importance to my question, "Did my wife go out?"

"Yes, sir, an hour ago, with another lady who came asking after her this morning, a few minutes after you left, sir."

A terrible suspicion crossed my mind.

"A lady!" I repeated. "What lady?"

"I don't know, sir, I've never seen her in Oran; she's a foreigner."

"Ah, a foreigner! You mean a Frenchwoman?"

"That may well be. In any case, she's not from here."

"And this lady," I continued, trembling, "is no doubt young, pretty, and blond?"

"Oh, no, sir! She is probably around forty years old and has very dark hair."

I took a breath.

"She looked to me," the bellboy added, "like a chambermaid."

He had scarcely uttered these words when I dashed away. I entered my suite and ran into Paule's room.

Nothing seemed to indicate a departure: her dresses were hanging in their usual place, her underclothes folded in the dresser, her trunk was resting in a corner. Clearly, my fears were ridiculous. She had gone out with some person from the city, a merchant woman, no doubt. She would come back.

I went into the drawing room, which I had only passed through, and to the mantel to see what time it was. A piece of paper, placed in front of the base of the clock, caught my eye.

It was a note, written hastily by Paule.

It contained only these words: "I have to leave you for a few days. Forgive me, and be patient. I will come back, I swear to you."

I didn't take the time to reflect on the meaning of the note, I understood only one thing: that she had left and that I had to find her at any cost.

I rushed down the staircase of the hotel, crossed the lobby, and came out onto the public square. Seeing Ben-Kader dozing sadly on the sidewalk, I cried, "Come on, drive me."

"Where?" he asked as he got up.

"You told me that my wife had left. Which direction did she take?"

Not answering, he began to walk solemnly in the direction of the port.

I begged him to move more quickly, but to no avail. It was useless: he would not hurry.

Finally, he stopped in front of a house on the wharf and showed me a sign that read: "Today, Saturday, departure at ten o'clock for Gibraltar, of the *Oasis*, Captain Raoul."

I turned to Ben-Kader, and he stretched out his arm toward the ocean, saying, in a melancholy voice and with a tear in his eye, "Very far."

This pantomime was as eloquent as the longest discourse: Paule had embarked at ten on a steamship headed for Gibraltar, and noon had just struck.

Just as I was wondering what course of action to take, a high-ranking official of the maritime authority, whom I had met at the Café Soubiran, came up to me.

"What are you doing here?" he cried. "I thought you had left with your wife. I saw her get on the *Oasis* this morning, and I assumed that she was meeting you on board."

"There was a misunderstanding," I answered, "and now I am desperate. I am looking for the fastest possible way to get to Gibraltar."

"Good heavens! I don't know any expeditious way to do that. The next departure isn't until Saturday."

"Can't you go to Cartagena and then on to Gibraltar from there?"

"That route is not being used right now."

"Won't I be able to find some sort of craft that can get me across the strait? Think how worried my wife must be!"

"I understand, but the boats from Oran just don't make trips that far. On the other hand, if you were in Nemours . . ."

"In Nemours! Can't I get there?"

"It's far."

"How far?"

"About two hundred kilometers by the Tlemcen road; a hundred and twenty if you follow the coast."

"Is it possible to follow the coast?"

"Perfectly possible, on horseback, as long as that doesn't scare you."

"I lived in Egypt for a long time and am used to that kind of travel."

"So do you want me to map out an itinerary for you?"

"You would be doing me a great service."

"You will need to hire a wagon driver, who will get you to the Andalusian plains in three hours' time. From there, you will go to Bou-Sfeur, to the house of a Spanish farmer, Pérès-Antonio. You will ask him for a guide and some horses, and he will provide them for you, especially if you remember to tell him I sent you."

"I will remember."

"Once you get to Nemours, while you're resting in the hotel, send for the captain of a balancelle. Balancelles are fairly solid vessels, half decked, manned by two or three men; they transport fruit from Gibraltar to Nemours and then go back with a load of ore. With a few coins, you can easily negotiate immediate passage on one of them, and if you don't waste a minute and the wind is in your favor, you should be able to arrive at your destination about twelve hours after the boat that left here this morning."

"I won't waste a minute!" I cried.

I thanked my guide warmly and took my leave of him.

By twelve thirty, I was en route to Nemours.

As I was leaving, Ben-Kader asked to come with me. I was worried about a sea voyage in difficult conditions for a child used to terra firma, and so declined his services. Fate was stalking me: I am now convinced that if I had yielded to the *yaouley*'s insistences, my enterprise would have turned out completely differently. You will understand later why I say that.

I suspect that you are not surprised, my friend, at my tenacity in following my wife, in spite of the difficulties the chase would entail and the promise contained in the note left at the hotel.

You already share my suspicions and terrors. The person who had found Paule that morning could be none other than Mme de Blangy's chambermaid, the same one who, the day we left Paris, had spoken for a moment with my wife at the door of the carriage.

How had that woman gotten to Oran? How had she even found out that we were in that particular city? Those things did not matter. It was obvious that she had been sent by Mme de Blangy, who had escaped from her husband's surveillance and was no doubt waiting for Paule in Gibraltar.

The first order of business was to catch up with them. I would decide later what to do after that.

XXV

I won't go into the details of the wild chase; they have been erased from my memory. I crossed villages, arid plains, rivers, and woods. My guide, although an Arab, had difficulty keeping up with me.

Thanks to the excellent directions that the maritime official had given me, I arrived in Nemours in the middle of the night.

To think that if I had hurried less, if, instead of entering a sleeping Nemours, I had walked its streets in broad daylight, I . . .

In just a moment, you will understand what I mean.

Having scarcely dismounted from my horse and giving no thought to rest, I headed for the port. I went into one of those bars that provide refuge, all night long, for sailors, and I didn't waste a minute negotiating my passage to Gibraltar with the captain of a balancelle.

At sunrise, we set sail. I wrapped myself up in an overcoat, stretched out at the stern, near the rudder, and at last was able to rest from my fatigue.

The weather was in our favor, and we had a brief and uneventful crossing.

Arriving in Gibraltar, I learned that the *Oasis*, docked in the port since the previous day, had not yet set sail again. I immediately set out to find the commanding officer of the steamship, Captain Raoul, a charming man whom Paule and I had had, several times, as a dinner companion at the Hôtel de la Paix.

He was on board; I found him.

He began the conversation the same way as the maritime official.

"What are you doing here?" he cried, as soon as he recognized me.

"Yes, I am here," I replied. "Doesn't it make sense for me to try to catch up with my wife? I missed the departure of the *Oasis*; she must have realized that and told you about it."

"My goodness, no! On the contrary, she told me that you preferred to get to Nemours overland. Since she is not at all frightened of the sea, she booked passage on my vessel, with her chambermaid, and had an excellent trip."

"Where is she now?"

"So that's it! You're playing hide-and-seek!" said the captain, laughing. "You make a plan to meet in Nemours, your wife disembarks there, while you . . ."

He was not able to finish his sentence.

"What?" I cried. "The *Oasis* stopped in Nemours?"

"Good Lord, yes! Whenever the weather permits it, we make a stop there. This time, more than ten people got off."

"And my wife was one of them?"

"Of course, dear sir; I obviously don't understand what's going on at all."

I understood, alas! And that was enough for me. I had just crossed the Mediterranean on a balancelle only to discover that my wife was in Nemours. I was strolling around in Spain, while she had remained in the province of Oran. The night before, I had probably walked down the street where she was staying; I may have stopped in front of her door to ask directions. Ah! If only I had had, as I was saying earlier, the good sense to wait until daybreak! If only I had brought Ben-Kader along with me, he would have guessed that she was in the city, or at least, during our trip on horseback, he would have had the chance to tell me that the *Oasis*, before crossing the strait, makes a stop on the coast. The maritime official, in my brief conversation with him, had not bothered to give me that piece of information, which he must have thought would be of no use to me: wasn't the steamship going to arrive at Nemours well before I could possibly get there?

Now I had to retrace my steps. Since the *Oasis* was not going back out to sea for another three days, Captain Raoul advised me to return on the balancelle that had brought me to Gibraltar. It was still, according to him, the fastest way to cross the strait. I took his advice. But the wind that had been in my favor when I was traveling away from Paule worked against me when I was going toward her. As in ancient times, the elements themselves conspired against me.

After a most painful crossing, I got back to Nemours one week after I had left it.

It was not hard to obtain the information about Paule I wanted. I was shown the house where she had stayed with a woman friend of hers, a Frenchwoman who had waited for her for some time and then left with her the day after I left Nemours. The two female travelers, accompanied by a chambermaid, had, I was assured, headed in the direction of Oran, by the Tlemcen road; they must have gotten there at least five days ago.

Would you believe it, dear friend? I did not rush to catch up with them. In the week that had just gone by, anger, indignation, and the intensity of the struggle had kept me going. Now, my nerves relaxed, anger gave way to tenderness, and I succumbed to an immense physical and moral lassitude. "Why hurry?" I asked myself. "Chance is guiding me, fate is hunting me down!"

I let go of the reins on my horse's neck and let him walk at his own pace. Gently rocking in my saddle, my eyes half closed, I had strange hallucinations. I heard Mme de Blangy's voice, she was sharply reproaching

Paule for having gone with me, for having stayed so long in Oran without trying to find her. She was telling her, "You prefer him to me now; his affection has replaced mine. But I will tear you away from his love. We will run away, far away, very far; they will never find us."

"No!" Paule was crying. "Go away! Go away! You're the one who ruined me! I want to be with him again, him . . . He taught me honesty and duty. He's waiting for me, he's suffering, he's calling out for me. I am leaving."

"Well then, I will go with you. But if he has not been waiting for you, it's because he does not love you, it's because he has deceived you, and then I will take you with me."

I imagined them arriving in Oran: Paule ran to the hotel; I was not there. At that point Mme de Blangy became more insistent: she spoke to her of the ten years that had gone by, and of the solemn oaths made in the convent and renewed later on. She evoked all the memories that linked them to each other. She hypnotized her, in a sense, by her words, forged a new link in the long chain of their memories and dragged her far away from me, bewildered, dying.

That is what I heard, that is what I saw during the journey of one hundred and twenty kilometers across the desert, and here is what was waiting for me in Oran.

A letter from Paule. I copy it here word for word:

"I am a wretched creature. But you must know how everything came about. I don't want to be accused of lies and duplicity. You have more than enough other wrongdoings

190

to reproach me for. I was sincere, I was truthful, during my stay here. At least hold on to the memory of that.

"As we were leaving Rue Caumartin, *her* chambermaid sneaked up to me and said, 'Madame is leaving with her husband. She knows that you are leaving too and has ordered me to let you know that everything will be all right and to follow you.' This woman, without your realizing it, got onto that express train to Marseilles; but once we went aboard ship, I didn't see her again, and if I had not been convinced that she had lost our trail, I would have asked you two months ago, I swear to you, if we could leave Oran.

"As for *her*, after arriving in Ireland, she slipped out from under her husband's surveillance one day, took off, and found her chambermaid in Paris, who informed her about us. She took off again immediately, crossing France, Spain, and the Mediterranean and debarking at Nemours. She wrote to me and begged me to join her; she claimed to be sick, and swore that she would keep me only for a day. After resisting for a long time, I went, swearing to you that I would be back. I kept my oath, I came back with every intention of seeking refuge with you, of asking you for help and protection against myself. I found that you were no longer here . . . Why didn't you wait for me? Why did you abandon me? Why did you leave me at her mercy? I am so weak and cowardly around her! You scorn me . . . I repulse you . . . you don't want to see me anymore. Oh, I understand how you feel . . . I understand, but I was becoming a better person, I swear to you, I was being born again to a new life, great progress was taking place inside me. But it was not finished yet; I was not yet strong enough, or purified enough, or regenerated enough, to resist bad advice. Hadn't I dared admit to you what kind of power she had over me? how she dominated me? how she had subjugated me? I didn't want to leave . . . I wanted to wait for you. But you didn't come back . . . I didn't know what had become of you. And I was afraid of you, I said to myself, 'Will he forgive me again?' I didn't dare hope for it . . . And *she* was always near, always at my side; she reproached me for my weakness, my cowardice, she said . . . Oh, I will say no more, no more! I shouldn't even speak to you about her. She has finally convinced me and I am leaving . . . going wherever she leads me . . . I have no idea where . . . What difference does it make where I go to hide my shame? . . . I am a fallen creature, a lost creature . . . I am less than nothing and I will never stand upright again . . . You see, you undertook an impossible task. We were both deluding ourselves. It's better that things end like this. I have ruined your life, you who are so good, so decent, so upstanding! Do not look for me . . . you will not be able to find me . . . She will know how to hide me better than you did . . . And I don't *want* to see you again! I would not dare look at you or speak to you after having treated you like this, when you were so generous with me! . . . Why, since we have been here, have you not spoken to me of your love, as you used to? There were no more bolts on my door . . . But you were still hurt by my past, you still scorned me, and I was waiting for time to regenerate me, to be worthy of you . . . What a mistake we made! Today, there would be indissoluble bonds between us that no one, no one could break . . . Good-bye, good-bye, forget me, pity me . . . If only you were to come back while I was writing this letter, I would throw myself at your feet, I . . . Hold on, I will wait until tomorrow; she can say what she wants, I will not leave until tomorrow. But come, come soon."

She had reopened her letter and written, "I have waited two more days . . . What has become of you? You have gone back to France. You have abandoned me. I am leaving. Good-bye, good-bye."

I read this letter two or three times, mechanically, as if in a daze; I felt pain all over my body, my head was heavy, and my teeth were chattering.

I took to my bed. A rather violent fever, accompanied by delirium, came over me in the night. The next morning, the hotel staff, not seeing me come down, came up to my room and hurried to send for Doctor X. For several days, he despaired of being able to cure me. Finally, he succeeded in conquering the illness: typhoid fever, I think.

XXVI

In the early days of January, I was able to set out for France. I was still very weak, but the long illness had allowed me to get some emotional rest. There had been a pause in my life, a sort of break that must have been good for me. I remembered, of course, all the events that had taken place, but I thought about them without bitterness, without annoyance, only with a great sadness. I was in a lot of pain, but my pain was not at all acute; it was latent, so to speak, smoldering secretly as a fire covered with ashes smolders: it burns but puts forth no flame.

I did, however, experience intense emotion when I returned to my apartment on Rue Caumartin. A thousand memories came flooding into my heart. I cried for a long time, a very long time.

When I was stronger, I put aside all the things that belonged to Paule and had them taken to her mother's house.

At the same time, I wrote to M. Giraud, "Your daughter has left me, sir. I do not know where she has sought refuge and I do not want to know. I would be grateful if you were never to ask me about her. I am sure you will understand that I wish to forget."

I knew that M. de Blangy was in Paris, but I made no attempt to see him. He exercised the same circumspection.

Nonetheless, we did meet one day on the boulevards. He approached me first, eagerly, and held out his hand. "I am happy," he said, "to find you in good health. I was afraid you might be ill."

"I was ill, gravely ill even," I responded. "I am better now . . . in every way," I added. "And yourself?"

"I have never felt better."

We didn't speak for a moment. It was the count who broke our silence.

"It would perhaps be prudent for us not to talk about the past. But you must agree that would be difficult. Between the two of us, any conversation that did not have to do with . . . our adventures . . . would immediately turn banal."

"That's probably true."

"All right then, let's go ahead and speak frankly . . . What an unfortunate campaign we undertook!"

"Quite unfortunate."

"She caught up with you?"

"Yes, in Africa. What can I say? I hadn't anticipated the possibility of her having us followed by her chambermaid."

I told the count all the details of my trip and my stay in Oran. I summed up Paule's letter in a few words.

"Yes," he said, after listening to me attentively, "your wife is worth more than mine. That is not, however, saying much."

For his part, he informed me of all the twists and turns of his trip in northern Europe.

"Once Mme de Blangy realized," he said, with a detached tone that left no doubt about the completeness of his recovery, "that she absolutely had to come with me, she complied quite gracefully."

"'What an excellent idea you had to come back!' she cried again and again. 'You just couldn't be nicer. And I have been wanting so much to travel! So we'll go to the north . . . oh, how happy I am! How awful of you not to have had this idea earlier! I was so bored in Paris! And you know, my dear, your travels around the world have done you a lot of good. You look younger. Why, you don't look a day over thirty! Here I am falling madly in love with you all over again!'"

"The truth is, I might have believed her," M. de Blangy continued, "if I hadn't known for a long time how extremely dishonest she was and if I hadn't figured out her scheme. Would you like to hear what the scheme was? (We have no secrets from each other, do we? What's more, why should I respect the privacy of that creature, to whom I no longer have any obligation whatsoever?) She was playing Delilah to my Samson. Throughout the trip, she smothered me with love, in order to be able to hand me over to the Philistines—that is to say, to run away from me, without my even considering running after her. With her admirably sharp mind, she had understood that I had not loved her for a long time, that my heart had nothing to do with my return to her, but that my imagination, still excited by the memory of a ten-month liaison suddenly broken off, demanded satisfaction.

"Mme de Blangy was adaptable enough to be able to calm even the most excited imagination; she succeeded in satiating mine. When she left me one evening in Dublin, I experienced, I swear to you, a great feeling of well-being.

I never would have thought to chase after her, if I hadn't remembered my commitment to you.

"That commitment proved to be impossible to uphold, though, and you will laugh when you hear the trick she played on me. It's worthy of her. When she left me, she took my wallet, which had all my money in it; I found myself, as the vulgar expression goes, *flat broke*, at the hotel. I had to write to France and ask for funds. They arrived a week later, at the same time as my wallet: Mme de Blangy had sent it back to me (without having opened it, I have to give her that), telling me that she was safe and that now I could come after her.

"Perhaps I was somewhat less zealous than I should have been in the whole matter, dear sir; do not hold that against me, I had no strength left for the fight. The idea for our double-pronged trip was yours. I do not reproach you for it, but let me tell you today that it was an unfortunate one.

"I have returned to my occupations in Paris, and if ever one of my colleagues at the ministry or at the club were to have the ill-advised idea of reminding me that there still exists, somewhere in the world, a Mme de Blangy, I would have the honor of immediately sending him my seconds. Two or three affairs of that sort would be enough to convince all my acquaintances that I am a widower. If I may permit myself to give you a piece of advice, dear sir, as I leave you, it would be for you to impose your status as premature widower on all your friends as well."

Several days after this conversation, dear friend, I had the pleasure of running into you in that house on Avenue Friedland.

I was, at the time, hungry for distraction; as I have already written, I was hoping that the activity and the noise would provide some diversion from my melancholy. But I found myself sadder and more discouraged than ever the day after the party. I did not even have the strength to show up at the meeting you and I had arranged, and I left, that same day, to travel.

Back in Paris, in June, I was in my study one morning, when I was told that Mme Giraud was asking to speak to me.

"Show her in," I said, after a moment of hesitation.

"You begged my husband never to talk to you about Paule," Paule's mother said to me, when she had sat down. "We have respected your wish, and both of us have wept in silence over the tragedy that struck you and, in so doing, injured us as well. We would continue to respect your wish today, if we did not have to keep a promise that has been wrenched out of us: Paule is sick, very sick, almost dying. She has asked us to let you know about her condition and to beg you to come say good-bye to her."

As soon as I could overcome the emotion clutching my heart, I asked Mme Giraud if her daughter was in Paris.

"No," she said, wiping away her tears, "she is living in Z., a little village in Normandy, on the seacoast; it takes only a few hours to get there."

I simply replied, "I will go."

Mme Giraud rushed toward me, took my hands in hers, and cried, "Oh, thank you, thank you! What joy you will bring to her! I do not know what wrongdoing she committed toward you. I saw her myself only three days ago . . . We had been informed in a letter that she was deathly ill, and I ran to her side. Can a mother possibly not forgive her dying child? She said nothing to me about the reasons for your separation; in fact, she would not have had the strength to, and I didn't have the heart to interrogate her. But I understood, from her desire to see you, from her repentance, that all the fault was on her side . . . Oh, forgive her, sir, forgive her, let her have that consolation to take with her when she dies!"

"But aren't you exaggerating the situation?" I said. "Is there no hope of saving her?"

"No," she answered. "I spoke with the doctor that she had sent for from Paris. He didn't know that I was her mother and gave me the true facts: she has a brain disease, the name of which I can't recall."

"Pachymeningitis," I said mechanically.

Suddenly I remembered Doctor X's terrifying prognosis . . .

"Yes, that's it," said the poor woman. "Her memory gets weaker every day, her thoughts are not clear at all anymore; she is barely able to find the words she needs. At night, she falls into a deep stupor, in which she is neither asleep nor awake and where she hears voices that speak to her and threaten her. She is extremely weak. Yesterday, to reassure me, she wanted to get up from the chaise longue she is always lying on, but her legs refused to support her."

The poor woman stopped there. She was sobbing and could not go on.

When she had calmed down, I promised her that I would leave that very day and asked her for the details I would need to find the house Paule was living in.

"Before you arrive in Z.," she said, "a short distance from the village, ask for Mme de Blangy's cottage."

"Mme de Blangy!" I cried, unable to suppress my indignation.

She looked at me, thought she understood, and said, "You are probably angry at her; she was my daughter's friend and should have kept her from falling short of her duties. Perhaps she didn't know anything about it; there are certain secrets that one does not confide, even to one's best friend. But please don't let that stop you from keeping your promise. You will not cross paths with Mme de Blangy, I didn't lay eyes on her a single time while I was in Z. She avoided me and will no doubt avoid you too."

Mme Giraud had scarcely left when I began preparing for my departure. The next morning, after a night spent on the train, I took a carriage to Z.

The cottage where Mme de Blangy had sought to be alone with Paule was located halfway up the wooded hills next to the cliff. My coachman pointed it out to me; I stepped down from the carriage and, in order to avoid any undesirable encounter, sent a local fisherman to inform my wife of my arrival.

Fifteen minutes later, I was in her room.

Mme Giraud had not been exaggerating: Paule was as ill as it is possible to be.

She did have the strength, though, to hold out her withered hand, which I kissed. Then she said:

"It's a good thing you came today . . . tomorrow would have been too late . . ."

The effort wore her out, and she closed her eyes.

I looked at her in silence; she was just a shadow of her former self. I had never realized people could change so much.

Great teardrops fell from my eyes onto her hand. Realizing that I was crying, she said, "Thank you."

Each time her lips opened a bit, I thought she was going to speak, but she was not up to it.

That night, she fell prey to the hallucinations that her mother had told me about. She seemed to be struggling with a ghost that she tried to push away with her hands, only to have it constantly return. Hoarse cries escaped from her throat. Sometimes, when I leaned over her, I could hear her murmuring fragments of sentences:

"Go away . . . go away, you wretch! . . . ruined . . . I'm afraid . . . I'm afraid . . . him, him!"

The next morning was calmer. Lying on her chaise longue in front of the window, she opened her eyes from time to time and looked far away in the direction of the ocean.

At one point, I was afraid that the bright sunshine might tire her and I went to close the curtains. She saw my gesture and murmured:

"No, no, leave them . . . The view is good for me . . . it makes me think that I'm still down there, with you, in Oran."

Around noon, her mother arrived from Paris, with the doctor who had come to Z. three days earlier.

He drew near his patient, said he thought he saw some improvement in her condition, and asked if his prescription to give her a bit of food had been followed.

"Only some soup" was the answer.

"That's not enough. Above all else, she needs sustenance. If she continues to do well between now and this evening, we will try to get her to take a nutritional puree that I will prepare myself."

When the doctor left, Paule gestured me to her side.

I obeyed.

"He's right," she said, "I do feel better today . . . How good you are to have come! . . . Two months ago, when I got sick, I wanted to write you, but I did not dare . . . I be-haved so badly . . . Ah! Now I am being punished for it . . . truly punished . . . Please forgive me."

She paused and began again a few seconds later: "You won't leave me, will you? . . . You will stay here, next to me, with my mother . . . You won't let anyone come in . . . And if I die, you will take my body back to Paris . . . I don't want to be buried here . . . Absolutely not! Absolutely not!"

Several minutes later, there were noises coming from the room next door, and I jumped up. She saw me get up and said, "Don't worry . . . she wouldn't dare come in . . . I forbade her to . . . I was not able to live with you, but I at least want to die in your arms."

Around five o'clock, we felt obliged to obey the doctor's orders and to give her the food that had been prepared especially for her.

We thought she would wave it away. What happened instead was a phenomenon often seen in patients suffering from the disease Paule had.

Suddenly her appetite came back, and she took the food being offered to her and quickly put it in her mouth.

Alas, the food stuck in her paralyzed throat. Her eyes became bloodshot, her face turned purple. She died of asphyxiation.

───────────

According to her wishes, I had her body sent back to Paris, and the burial took place three days later at the Père-Lachaise Cemetery.

In September of that same year, M. de Blangy read with keen interest the following newspaper article:

"The little beach at Z. was the setting yesterday for a most tragic scene. Mme de Blangy—a charming woman from the best of families and an intrepid swimmer as well—has been living in our area since the beginning of the season. She had just taken a stroll along the cliffs, accompanied by one of her friends, Mlle B., that ravishing young brunette we noticed at the last ball at the casino, when it occurred to her that she would like to take a swim. She was told that the tide was going out, that in this season of heavy tides, strong currents could easily drag her out to sea, and that at the moment there was no lifeguard on the beach to come to her rescue.

"'No matter!' she said. 'I can take care of myself perfectly well without any help.'

"She had a cabana opened for her, from which she soon emerged in an elegant bathing suit and headed determinedly for the water.

"Within several strokes, she was in open water.

"'Come back, come back!' they cried from the beach.

"But she did not listen and continued to swim, shouting with laughter every now and then, which reassured her friends.

"Soon, however, it appeared that she had been carried off farther than she wanted to go; the current seemed to be dragging her away.

"'Help, help!' cried the tearful Mlle B.

"At that moment, M. Adrien de C. arrived on the beach.

"Upon inquiring, he was told what was happening.

"'Ah!' he exclaimed. 'It's Mme de Blangy!'

"He immediately removed some of his clothes and plunged into the water.

"The woman he was trying to save, at the very risk of his own life, was none other than the best friend of the young wife he lost just last June, a wife whom he still misses so much that he has not been able to bring himself to leave our area.

"He soon caught up to Mme de Blangy. In spite of the distance, they could be seen struggling for quite a while. It appeared as if there was an actual battle going on between the two of them. Like all drowning people, Mme de Blangy was no doubt trying desperately to clutch on to her rescuer, who pushed her away in order to have the necessary freedom of movement . . . The current continued to drag them out, and soon they vanished from sight.

"Ten minutes went by . . . ten minutes that seemed like a century! M. Adrien de C. reappeared . . . Alas! he was alone . . . he had been unable to save the poor woman and had had barely enough strength to make it back to the beach himself."

Having read the article, M. de Blangy picked up his pen and wrote:

"I understand what happened, and I thank you, on my own behalf and on behalf of all decent people, for having rid us of that reptile . . . The danger in which you placed yourself serves as your absolution."

He then folded the letter in half and had it delivered to M. Adrien de C., Rue Caumartin.

Modern Language Association of America
Texts and Translations

Texts

1. Isabelle de Charrière. *Lettres de Mistriss Henley publiées par son amie.* Ed. Joan Hinde Stewart and Philip Stewart. 1993.
2. Françoise de Graffigny. *Lettres d'une Péruvienne.* Introd. Joan De-Jean and Nancy K. Miller. 1993.
3. Claire de Duras. *Ourika.* Ed. Joan DeJean. Introd. Joan DeJean and Margaret Waller. 1994.
4. Eleonore Thon. *Adelheit von Rastenberg.* Ed. and introd. Karin A. Wurst. 1996.
5. Emilia Pardo Bazán. *"El encaje roto" y otros cuentos.* Ed. and introd. Joyce Tolliver. 1996.
6. Marie Riccoboni. *Histoire d'Ernestine.* Ed. Joan Hinde Stewart and Philip Stewart. 1998.
7. Dovid Bergelson. *Opgang.* Ed. and introd. Joseph Sherman. 1999.
8. Sofya Kovalevskaya. *Nigilistka.* Ed. and introd. Natasha Kolchevska. 2001.
9. Anna Banti. *"La signorina" e altri racconti.* Ed. and introd. Carol Lazzaro-Weis. 2001.
10. Thérèse Kuoh-Moukoury. *Rencontres essentielles.* Introd. Cheryl Toman. 2002.
11. Adolphe Belot. *Mademoiselle Giraud, ma femme.* Ed. and introd. Christopher Rivers. 2002.

Translations

1. Isabelle de Charrière. *Letters of Mistress Henley Published by Her Friend.* Trans. Philip Stewart and Jean Vaché. 1993.
2. Françoise de Graffigny. *Letters from a Peruvian Woman.* Trans. David Kornacker. 1993.
3. Claire de Duras. *Ourika.* Trans. John Fowles. 1994.
4. Eleonore Thon. *Adelheit von Rastenberg.* Trans. George F. Peters. 1996.
5. Emilia Pardo Bazán. *"Torn Lace" and Other Stories.* Trans. María Cristina Urruela. 1996.
6. Marie Riccoboni. *The Story of Ernestine.* Trans. Joan Hinde Stewart and Philip Stewart. 1998.

7. Dovid Bergelson. *Descent*. Trans. Joseph Sherman. 1999.
8. Sofya Kovalevskaya. *Nihilist Girl*. Trans. Natasha Kolchevska with Mary Zirin. 2001.
9. Anna Banti. *"The Signorina" and Other Stories*. Trans. Martha King and Carol Lazzaro-Weis. 2001.
10. Thérèse Kuoh-Moukoury. *Essential Encounters*. Trans. Cheryl Toman. 2002.
11. Adolphe Belot. *Mademoiselle Giraud, My Wife*. Trans. Christopher Rivers. 2002.